Welcome to Wibble Street: The Magpie Has Landed

Andrew William

DEDICATION

For all the children I have ever had the privilege of teaching.

CONTENTS

ACKNOWLEDGMENTS

Mum and Dad

Calum and Katie

Shobnall Primary School

The many children who reviewed sections of the book

The Year 5/6 Class of The British School of Geneva (2011/12)

Front cover by Amy Bradley

A Crow Lands

Alarm bells were ringing out over the sky of Skaggyness town, as George Forest ('the most red headed small boy in Skaggyness – and that is official,' according to his Uncle Edwin) was kicking his football against the wall at the front of his house. "Oops!" he mumbled to himself as he kicked the ball accidentally against the bright red front door of number one Wibble Street.

He paused for thought as he listened to the sirens piercing the air of the town. The buzzing of a helicopter approaching overhead, with the throbbing alarms, mixed a cocktail of danger that was packing the Skaggyness air.

He wondered what was causing such panic. He gained a hard hitting clue as he looked down the street, hand shading his eyes from the Sun, towards the noise of the sirens that were rapidly getting closer.

Terror, clutching a bag of something, was pelting down Wibble Street towards him. The running man was adorned with a black woolly hat clutching his head tightly. His breathing was so heavy he was in competition from the swirling surround sound of the circling helicopter. The heavy pounding of his feet from his ample frame added to growing thoughts of danger for George, who had now become transfixed with wonder. He stared like a statue at the horror that seemed to be thundering towards him.

As the man smelled ever closer, George could see him sweating furiously. The figure was unshaven, sporting a scar all across his left-cheek. A police car turned into the end of the street in pursuit of the man dressed in a black running suit. George suddenly considered that it might be a good idea to hide as anyone else in the street had briskly disappeared indoors.

The man made momentary eye contact with George as his movement was passing him. Without thought or intent George panicked as he tried to turn and run to hide behind the small wall at the front of the

1

garden. The red headed supremo fell over his ball and in his desperate scramble kicked the ball backwards. The ball was sent perfectly into the hole of the stride of the mysterious figure hot footing it from somewhere to somewhere. George and the running man hit the ground at the same time. George was behind the wall hands tucked into the grass, sniffing daisies. The running man had hit the pavement with a thud and was groaning wildly cursing George describing him as a little so and so. George has clearly heard the bag the man was carrying spill onto the floor sending the man's personal valuable coin collection all over the street.

'Don't hurt me, please don't hurt me!' George muttered to himself. The now moaning man had hurt himself in the fall and stumbled again as he tried to get to his feet. George's ball had found its way into the road and bounced back into the gutter as a police car pulled sharply up by the man's snot ridden nose.

A second police car screeched to a halt from the round the opposite direction as the two police cars converged surrounding the very spot the aching, panting man had fallen.

George listened intently to the conversation, not daring to show himself from the other side of the wall. He could clearly hear the police telling the man he could keep quiet or say something that they would use in court, the choice was his. The police bundled him into the back of the first car to arrive as the police argued which officer was going to make the arrest. The arrested man was screaming his head off swearing revenge on 'the little so and so behind the wall'. The man protested greatly that he was in great pain due to his fall but the police simply pushed him in the back of the car with him nicely cuffed. "Police brutality, police brutality!" he bellowed but no one was around to care.

George was scared of policemen, almost as much as he was scared of sweaty, unshaven, scarred, large men dressed in black running away from the sound of danger and who had racing police cars coming after him. His father was always threatening to send him down to the police station if he ever did anything wrong so he was rather startled to feel the shadow of a uniformed officer lurking over him requesting him to stand-up. As George stood and dusted his red tracksuit down attempting to make himself as smart as the two officers of the law he was now facing.

"You're a hero young man!" announced the lady officer.

"Am I?" George responded.

"Oh yes you are young man," the policeman with her confirmed.

"What's your name little hero?" the lady officer asked.

"J-J-J-J-George," he mumbled nervously and he grinned half-a-grin.

"Well George, somehow you've helped us catch Mickey Magpie," smiled the female officer.

"Mickey Magpie?" George said in bewilderment.

"Only one of the notorious Crow Gang who have just robbed the Central Bank in town," the male officer added.

"Did Mickey Magpie mean it when he said he would be back to kill me?" George asked with real concern.

"Probably," the male officer mumbled to the ground nodding his head as the policeman knew full well the Crow Gang were capable of anything. They were wanted all over the country for so many crimes from shoplifting to bank robbery as well as kidnap and murder. In short, the Crow Gang were capable of all and any dastardly deeds. The Crow Gang were always happy to make people suffer in any way they could!

The lady officer threw her arm out to stop the male police officer from saying any more and tried to reassure George that he was perfectly safe. "Oh, you are quite alright we have him now and he will be safely tucked up in a cell within the hour," she said.

The two officers enquired as to where his parents were as they would like to commend him as a hero but George explained he was being looked after by his next door neighbour, Mrs Diamond, as his parents were both at work. The uniformed duo then got a call over the radio and quickly fled from George's side.

The police cars disappeared and the ball had been thrown back into the garden of number one. George picked-up his ball and pondered whether he was comfortable being a hero or not. He thought he might become a super hero with his football as a weapon to foil crime!

Then George remembered how the man had cursed him and knew exactly where he lived and with his distinctive red hair there would be no-way he would be able to stop Mickey Magpie or any of the Crow Gang from getting revenge on him. 'No, not happy,' thought George.

After confirming his uncomfortable position as a hero to himself, just moments later he was stroking a friendly white horse that had clipped-clopped from the direction of the running man. The horse was well known round Skaggyness. No-one ever bothered or thought anything of this quite magnificent beast roaming around the town as it pleased. The people of Skaggyness called the horse 'Random' and 'Random' was a regular visitor to George's shoulder. A warm welcome and a friendly pat secured a bonding kinship for two spirits who often felt more than their fair share of loneliness.

George stroked Random and spoke to him; "Hello Random! What you been up to today then?" Random was soon off again and disappeared around the corner of Wibble Street. The steed was soon heading down Twilight Street following where the police cars had gone before it.

George was called in by his mum, who George had been adamant with the police was not home. He was told to get upstairs to tidy his room, which he duly did without complaint. He was told his room must be tidy by the time she returned from the shops but he had done it in two minutes. George's room was never that bad and when he had finished he jumped on his bed and lay reading a book about the planets. He was imagining he was rocketing to a place in space on a mission of discovery with a team of experts who would discover all the answers to the problems of the universe.

George had lived at number one Wibble Street, Skaggyness, for all of his young years. Wherever he went he was noticed, mainly due to his freckled face and flaming red hair. He lived in the corner house of the street and spent most of his time playing on his own. It was never really clear whether George was a happy ten-year old chap or not as he didn't make friends easily. Most of the children he knew lived on the other side of the town then one fine and bright August morning, with the school holidays in full flow, a new family moved into number eleven Wibble Street. They had moved into the house on the opposite corner to George's home.

George's Mum returned home from the shops within the hour, she never left George or his sisters on their own in the house for too long. Mrs Forest shouted up the stairs to George.

"Hi guys I'm home, do you want a drink?"

"Sure," George called down. His sisters shouted they had already got a drink, they were always happy to sort themselves out while George preferred to be mothered.

"Come down and get it then."

George thudded down the stairs leaping off the last two steps to land two-footed on the ground. He presented himself to his mum always looking for her approval and now looking for his drink. Mum poured him a milk and handed him a chocolate biscuit. George grinned with pleasure as his mum ruffled his hair. His two sisters (his elder sister Tracey and younger sister Stacey) were sitting there quietly drinking and munching ahead of him. George didn't really say a lot to his two sisters, they seemed to have each other and George was always the spare.

"That was all very exciting this morning wasn't it? All those alarms and sirens. Fancy the police catching the robber in Wibble Street. Did any of you guys see anything?" Mrs Forest enquired of the kitchen based audience.

"Apparently, the man was extremely dangerous but then you would be if you were a member of the Crow Gang, only the most wanted savage men in the country!" exclaimed Mrs Forest.

George decided not to mention to his mother he was a hero. He knew how his father always said the police were always in need of a wash. He didn't think they would believe him when he would tell them how he purposefully used his football to bring down in pain one of the most dangerous men in the country. After all, super heroes must keep their identity a secret. He decided that he would say absolutely nothing; his actions would remain a secret between himself and the police.

The children frantically shook their head in response to their mother's chat and George insisted he knew nothing as he was in some way trying to forget the words of Mickey the Magpie. George had noted that his family weren't all that rich. He made the assumption that they didn't qualify as wealthy so were probably safe from being robbed or kidnapped but worse than that for him he could not be sure of. However, George knew that Mickey Magpie was safely locked away and that he was not in any kind of danger while he was. His mum continued her chatting to the children who always listened to her words, unlike their father who clearly never listened or talked much to any of them.

"I passed number eleven on the way back from the shops, there's a new family moving in and they have a little boy, about your age," his mum told him.

"I know," George wheezed. "His name's Billy and he is going to be in our class at school."

"Why don't you go out and see if he wants to play with you," she suggested.

"Mum, he might be a bully or a daft person, best wait till he turns up at school and I can check him over, see if he is alright, and all that," said George, sharing his thinking.

George's mum also shared her observations with him, "Don't be silly, it's still weeks before term starts again. George, he looked perfectly fine to me. His mum stopped and said hello as I raced passed, she seemed very pleasant and I bet he is too."

"Drink your milk and eat your biccy and go and introduce yourself. I bet he would love to meet you," she said assuringly.

"He won't like me! They never really like me," insisted George.

"Just go and be nice and he will think your great," his mum said delightfully.

George stood there and downed his milk and quickly scoffed his biscuit, a little chocolate had scuffed onto the corner of his mouth, and his mum quickly wiped it for him as he lay down the glass on the table. He stood there waiting for his mum to stop tidying him up, she adjusted his red track suit top and pulled down his red t-shirt. His mum then adjusted his red track suit trousers and tied his red trainer laces on his red trainers which lay under and over his red socks.

"You'll do," announced his mum.

George bolted for the front door grabbing his red sports jacket on the way. He had made the decision to do as his mum had said as he was suddenly feeling confident about himself, a feeling he didn't carry with himself every day – 'I'm a super hero'- 'don't tell anyone' he thought to himself. He slammed the door, accidentally, behind him. The number one, which hung on the red front door, nearly leaped off with the power of the slam. He walked down the street towards number eleven, thinking as he slowly approached his new neighbour's home.

He wondered what he could say, how should he make a friend of this boy, would he like him, would he like him back? 'Be nice,' he thought, 'that's what mum said, and it would be great to have a mate in Wibble Street. I could show him around and tell him everything he needs to know.'

George was sure of himself now and he had pin-knobbed down to the street to arrive outside number eleven.

There he stood, in all his red splendour, watching the removal men shift the remaining furniture into number eleven. 'They're house is all blue, where ours is all red,' mused George. He stood for what seemed to him an age simply observing all the possessions of a family household entering the house. George played a game with himself as all the items disappeared into the home, 'downstairs, upstairs...as each article of household ware entered the building he gave his opinion to himself as to where he thought the article would go; 'upstairs, downstairs, upstairs'. A huge dusty lamp was marched in, 'definitely downstairs, could be bedroom though so maybe not.'

"Hi, what's your name?" asked the woman of the house.

"George," he replied sheepishly, blushing as he was surprised to be spotted and she had caught him off his guard.

"Well George, do you live close to here?" the woman inquired.

"Number one, the red house at the end, can't miss it," he said proudly.

The woman introduced herself and greeted George's claim with a warming smile, "Good, I am Mrs. Ranger and I have a little boy inside, my son, who would love to meet you. Would you like to meet him?"

"Ok," George replied casually with a slight shrug of his shoulder which disguised the excitement he was actually feeling inside. He had never had a friend in Wibble Street to have fun with before and he had the highest of hopes at this moment. Mrs. Ranger gestured to George to wait where he was as she went to the blue front door of number eleven. He could see the bottom of the stairs where she stood leaning her neck towards the top of the steps. She shouted for her son to come down. George stood waiting patiently wondering what this boy was going to be like, 'I will be his friend,' George promised himself. He had been impressed with Mrs. Ranger and figured the son would be just fine if he had such a lovely mum. A figure had now appeared at the foot of the stairs.

Mrs. Ranger had a quick word with the boy and then she ushered him outside with a gentle two-handed push and pointed towards George who was slightly grimacing as the figure approached. 'Something's not quite right but what?' quizzed George to himself.

The lad arrived in front of George and Mrs. Ranger looked on clasping her two hands together and noted with a look of anticipation the reactions of the two boys.

The new body spoke first, "I am Billy, pleased to meet you mate!"

"I am J-J-J...George... Ffff...Forest," George spluttered nervously.

They paused for a second or two and looked each other up and down. George stood there resplendently head-to-foot bathed in redness, including his blushing cheeks. Billy was precisely the same height as George and held himself as he began to check Billy out with a full commentary to them both as he did so.

"Blue trainers, blue laces, blue socks, blue trousers, blue t-shirt, blue jacket and blue hair! You've got blue hair!" gasped George in bewilderment.

"Genius! You worked all that out on your own tomato head!" countered Billy.

"Mates?" Billy thrust out his hand for George to take as his friend.

"Mates!" George grinned the broadest grin as he took Billy's hand for a manly shake and realised he had just made his first real pal in Wibble Street and he had the bluest of blue hair, cool!

Wibble Street

George was munching away on his breakfast cereal still curious as to how exactly a man called Mickey Magpie – a member of the apparently world infamous Crow Gang – should choose Wibble Street to run down. He thought about how his 'super powers' might show themselves next.

What was Mickey Magpie's history?

Would he really do the things he threatened?

What if the other gang members find out about him?

George didn't discuss anything with his family, he just hoped to survive each day, come home to his mum, the woman who fed him and hugged him.

George's big and little sister sat at the wooden breakfast table scoffing tea and toast. He never really said much to his sisters and they never said much to him. The three siblings never played together but they rarely argued either. His mum was tidying the kitchen but his dad was still in his bed. His mum was aware that he had made arrangements to meet his new friend that morning to show him around Wibble Street.

Wibble Street, a curious place in so many ways. George wondered what his new pal Billy would make of Wibble Street. As the family sat down eating their breakfast, but saying nothing, he pondered on what Billy might think of his new base, Skaggyness. Skaggyness was a coastal town and walking by the sea could be great fun. Maybe Billy had never lived by the sea before, surely he would love that? 'Brace yourself Billy, it's very breezy round here sometimes,' George imagined what he would say to describe Skaggyness to his new friend.

George slid off the polished wooden table chair and announced to the ladies of the house that he was off to meet his mate!

"Be careful love won't you?" his mum said lovingly.

"Have a good time but do be careful, I know what boys can be like when they get together," his mum said knowingly.

Anxiously, George shook his head.

"I am only going to show him Wibble Street and tell him things about Skaggyness," he answered as if slighted by the mere suggestion that he could get into any trouble.

There was a thudding above his head, a three-time thud. It was his dad.

Nervously, his mum said, "He must be awake. He will want a tea and his paper."

"You'd better see to him and I need to go my MATE's house," George boasted.

His two sisters said nothing but raised their fingers that were wrapped around their toast, signalling a wave goodbye.

George opened the red door at the front of the house opening on to Wibble Street. He breathed in a huge breath and noted what a gorgeous summer's day it was. He turned round and stooped to pickup his red cap and placed it carefully on his red head of hair. He was red-dy!

Really happily, he went out into Wibble Street and closed the door behind him. He turned to face the direction of number eleven and crouched down to tie his red training shoe laces. As he was busy tying the laces his next door neighbour, number two Wibble Street, Mrs Diamond was just setting out.

"Good morning young man. What are you up to today my handsome boy?" she said clearly very interested in the activities of her young neighbour.

Rapidly, he smiled and replied, "I am off to see my new mate. His name's Billy and he has moved into number eleven."

"Good, that's nice dear. Will you be getting into mischief the pair of you?" she asked with serious concern.

"No, not me Mrs Diamond," George assured her.

Sadly, Mrs Diamond said to him, "Just mind my flowers if you're playing your ball games, that's all I ask."

"Will do Mrs Diamond. I will guard them with my life," he accompanied his boast with a salute bringing his right hand up quickly to the peak of his red cap as he stood on tiptoes pushing his chest out. With his cheeks sucked in and his gaze fixed firmly dead ahead Mrs Diamond acknowledged his obedience. "At ease young man," she instructed him with a commanding tone.

Mrs Diamond now had an enormous grin on her face and fought wildly with herself not to burst out laughing at George's actions.

"I must get on now young man. I don't want to miss all the good stuff in the shops. Ta, ta for now," she said. Quickly, (or at least quick for a woman in her nineties) she shuffled on in the direction of the shops pulling her shopping basket behind her.

With utter joy, he proceeded to stroll in the opposite direction as he headed for number eleven. As he approached the house he passed every home in Wibble Street. He was reminding himself of everybody he knew who lived there.

He didn't actually know every person in the street, but he was sure he knew their faces. As he passed each house he recalled the few names he knew. As he reached half-way down the street there was loud music coming from the big white house - well actually it is two homes made into one - number six and number seven. He gulped a nervous breath and sprinted passed keeping his head down, he daren't place a glance towards the window of number six and seven.

He started to stroll again as he reached number eight and sure enough, a few seconds later, he arrived at his new chum's house. He tucked his red t-shirt into his red trousers before he rang the bell.

George reached up to the bell and stretched out to press the button down firmly.

To his surprise, music followed the release of the button.

'This ole' house once knew his children,

This ole' house once knew a wife,

This ole' house was home and comfort...'

Billy opened the door and greeted him.

"Ay up mate, how's it goin'?"

"Alright, you?" George replied.

Billy quickly turned round to announce his exit to his mum, "I am off mum, I'll be back when I'm starving!"

"I like your doorbell, it's cool!" George complimented.

Awkwardly, Billy explained, "It's my dad's idea of a joke, but you never know what it will play. He has downloaded his whole collection of ancient ditties on his new phone and rigged it up to the doorbell. So every time you press it you suffer one of his favourite excuses for music."

'Brilliant!' thought George, 'His dad must be really clever. My dad has only just learned how to get a CD to play never mind get the doorbell to act as an on button for a music show!' his thoughts raced.

Curiously, Billy asked, "What we up to then?"

"I thought I'd show you Wibble Street," said George slightly over excited.

Billy looked up and down the street and paused for a few seconds as he placed his left hand over his peepers to shield them from the sun.

"Okay, seen it! What's next?" he queried. Billy clocked the disappointed and bemused look on George's face.

"Only joking my old tomato head! Let's walk slowly and you can tell me all I need and want to know," announced Billy.

George showed an uneasy relief, for a second or two, he thought Billy was being unfriendly. George wasn't sure if he liked being called tomato head, he thought he wouldn't call him tomato head if he knew he had super powers that can flatten criminals.

"Let's cross the road and I can talk you through who is who in the street," George informed him.

Without hesitation, Billy asked, as he pointed firmly across to the huge white-washed mass that stretched menacingly parallel to the row of houses on the other side of the street, "Ok. First question, what on earth is the deal with that thing across the street?"

Neighbours

The two boys looked left and right down Wibble Street and raced across the road opposite number eleven. They both smacked into the huge white wall before them with their palms open and their faces were pressed against the brick work. As they tore themselves off the white wall they turned to face each other.

"What is this wall all about mate? Why it is here?" Billy pressed the issue which was clearly bothering him.

"Well it is just a wall," insisted George innocently.

"I have never seen anything like it," Billy claimed.

Billy continued, developing a stressful voice full of puzzlement, "It is huge. In all my long life I have never seen such a wall. I look to the left and I look to the right and I look up. All I can see is this humongous white wall. It stretches into the clouds. It never seems to end. Have you ever seen the end of the wall? What's behind it?" Billy was really anxious about the structure.

George thought carefully about Billy's questions and suddenly realised that he had never once questioned the existence of the white wall. The wall had always been there across the road from the houses on Wibble Street. George had always just accepted the existence of the wall and no houses, the wall enveloped the town and had truck wide gaps for the purposes of exit and entrance.

The wall was actually eight metres high and four metres thick, built from concrete. The wall was whitewashed with the brightest of white paint. When the small team of people had finished painting the whole wall they simply went round again…and again…and again…and so on!

"Never in my life have I lived in a place that is completely surrounded by a wall, a huge white wall. Why is it here? What's the point of it?" quizzed Billy.

Billy was hoping George would launch into a detailed and clear explanation of how the wall was originally built and why it was there.

Was it built by Saxons?

Was it built by The Romans and then kept and maintained for historical reasons?

The wall did seem quite modern in appearance. George responded to Billy's quiz, "Dunno!" Billy's heart sank, he loved to know everything about everything and it was soon clear that George didn't know much about anything!

Billy had now brought the life of the wall into debate. Suddenly George had no answers, what was behind the wall? George had no idea where the wall began or ended. George had always assumed that there was nothing behind the wall, just the edge of the world or something, he had simply never wondered hard enough to be bothered to find out.

George shared his thoughts with his new friend. Billy wanted to know more and suggested that they walked until they reached the edge of this snowy styled dividing force. George talked him out of it as he had promised his mum not to go too far that morning. He suggested to Billy that he had seen the wall at different points on the edge of Skaggyness. They would be in need of a car and a driver to stand any chance of a discovery.

"Another day then, but one day we will find the answer my friend!" promised Billy.

They were quiet for a few seconds as they started to amble alongside the wall towards George's house. The house stood deep in scarlet perched across the street like it was leaning on a lamp post on the corner of the street. They glanced at the houses across the road, which provoked comment and questions from Billy.

"Number ten? Our next door folk," enquired Billy wanting to know about the people he shares a street with.

"Dulkars, think they're foreign," said George. They are a big family, Sachin is in my class at school". Billy nodded soaking up the information but a little disappointed George couldn't tell him more.

"Number nine?" Billy continued his line of enquiry.

"It's a famous bloke who lives there. He is some kind of sportsman and the woman's made of plastic," George claimed.

"Really? Which sport is he famous for? Is she really made of plastic?" Billy queried George's assertion.

"Well I think he's with Skaggyness Albion, the football club, but she certainly looks like she's made of plastic! I have seen them both drive off in their black sports car, it's a pretty cool machine. I have also seen them in magazines and I think I saw them on the news once," George continued to inform his pal.

"Wow, pretty cool to have them in the street. I need more detail though George, I need names and details!" Billy demanded.

"What about number eight?" continued Billy.

George explained that he knew the faces of everyone in the street but didn't know many of their names. He was apologising to Billy and almost pleading for forgiveness from him. George felt that the lack of facts in his grand tour of the street had failed Billy miserably. After a while, Billy insisted that it didn't really matter and that they would make it their business to find out all about everybody and everything that happens in Wibble Street. George agreed and could see the anticipation of fun to come as he had never spent so much time with anybody who was so curious about anything and everything they came into contact with.

"Oh erm, watch for the people at numbers six and seven!" George quickly interjected.

"Why my old tomato head?"

In the blink of an eye, George launched into a panicky conversation about how the same family lived in both number six and number seven. He explained how they were the Burton family and that Mr and Mrs Burton lived at number six and all the children lived in bedrooms at number seven. "That's the not the bad bit!" continued George now getting into as bit of a state. "All the children are girls, it's the house of the seven sisters! Trust me now you don't want anything to do with them! They're all trouble! Sugar and spice all things nice, never been wronger with that lot! They're a wicked bunch and I want nothing to do with them!"

"I get your point!" said Billy, "You don't need to blow a gasket!"

Billy could see the fear on George's face, he was wiping the sweat pouring from his brow. Billy thought he looked like a scared seal dripping wet desperate to escape a chasing polar bear. Billy decided to stay quiet although he was burning with desire to find out more about what makes the seven sisters in Wibble Street so chilling.

The paper boy (who just happened to be a girl) was cycling down the street towards our blue and red boys. "Can you put that through at number six mate?" she smiled at Billy and handed the newspaper to him. Billy nodded at her, 'Course darlin' he said smiling and winking at her as he took the paper from her. The girl tossed her blonde locks back and smiled to herself laughing as she rode down the street to continue her round.

Billy decided he would take a quick look at the paper. He shared the headlines with George. "MAGPIE LANDS IN COURT AS CROW GANG FLY AWAY".

"That was wicked yesterday. If Skaggyness is like that every day it will be brilliant!" insisted Billy.

George was trying not to say anything as he was bursting to tell his role in the capture of Mickey Magpie. He figured Billy would not accept his super human role in the arrest of an infamous thug; after all he knew to be a real super hero he had to stay stum. George was quickly trying to scan the report for his name and an account of his super hero effort – but nothing! Not a mention of a little boy or a super hero with a football criminal felling weapon. The police claimed full credit for Mickey Magpie's capture.

"It says here that the Crow Gang are wanted in seventeen point three countries for loads of stuff they've done," read Billy sharing it with George as he tried to stretch his neck over to read the article with him.

The report stated that the police said that the gang escaped and went off in different directions. 'The Crow Gang are at large and are believed to be armed and dangerous'.

"Armed and dangerous! Gosh we could be in right bother if we meet that lot! I wouldn't want to be in the shoes of anyone who upsets the Crow Gang!" Billy vented.

George went pale at the thought of Mickey Magpie's threats and the idea that there was a whole gang of these ugly sounding bandits.

"The police reckon that the Gang got away with over half-a-million pounds! They'll be long gone by now!" Billy predicted.

"Good! Long gone! Like it!" chipped in George.

Billy folded the paper after a quick glance at the sport on the back page. He posted it as promised through number six only to be greeted with lots of barking. Not ordinary dog barking but what Billy thought was a lot of human barking, followed by girls laughter as they had probably been amused by the slightly stunned look on Billy's face. Billy remembered what George had said about number six and seven.

George continued his World Tour of Wibble Street, though couldn't say anything about the people in number eight, number five or number four. He explained all about Mrs Diamond at number two and that a teacher from their school, Mr Horn, lived at number three.

"I think he lives on his own, Mr Horn at number three that is," George supplied quality information for Billy this time.

"Erm," Billy was listening and nodding to any crumb of data he could give him.

"But there's often strange noises that come from the house".

"Really?" Billy pressed for more.

"Strange noises," George stressed.

It's an interesting street thought Billy. A collection of mysteries and people to find out about he noted.

Billy couldn't resist revisiting the issue of the House of the Seven Sisters and wanted to know specific things they had done that had caused George so much fear.

"Well I don't know what to say. Just whatever you do not ever make eye contact with any of the children from that house," George said with a tremble in his voice.

"How not?" Billy pressed.

"They're a very scary bunch!" George claimed.

"How thrilling. A dangerous crew. Are they our age? How many of them are they?" Billy continued.

"I beg of you keep your head down and walk away, have nothing to do with them. They eat boys for breakfast. I am convinced they eat lads for Sunday dinner when people I know have a slaughtered cow, chicken or sheep."

George was begging Billy to avoid any contact with the girls in the house insisting they were animals and were a very dangerous crew. Billy expressed the fact that he couldn't believe that George was so petrified of a bunch of silly girls.

"Silly girls! They're a deadly bunch Billy, be careful with them they're more scary than anybody I know," insisted George, although Mickey Magpie had probably overtaken them in the 'scariest people I know' bar chart he once completed in maths.

Billy was thinking about all the exciting challenges he had discovered on his new door step and he was buzzing inside with exhilaration. He had never anticipated that he would be moving to such a curious avenue. He promised George he wouldn't seek out an eyeball with the girls, at least not today anyway.

"Can I meet your family?" asked Billy.

"Erm, well, okay. Do you mean now?" George asked.

"Yes, if that's okay," said Billy.

George was a bit reluctant and seemed to stall a meeting with his family. Billy started to wonder what the problem was, after all he had met his mum why shouldn't he meet Mrs Forest?

George said it would be okay but wasn't sure who would be in. He advised Billy to keep his head down and not to look up as they passed by number seven. It all seemed a bit too much for George. Billy thought he had better do it, if only to please his new friend. So they both walked quickly passed the house of the Seven Sisters staring at the pavement. George took a sharp intake of breath and held it in until he had safely passed number seven and six. They crossed over the road towards George's home and met Mrs Diamond outside number two returning from the shops.

He introduced Billy to his next door neighbour. She was always kind to George and he treated her like she was his own grandmother. Mrs Diamond talked to the boys for a minute or two while George recounted almost every detail of what they had both been doing since the very moment he had left Mrs Diamond a full hour and more earlier. She patiently waited for George to run out of steam as he energetically jumped around. He was very excited as he had been able to spend the morning with a friend and was beaming as he introduced one friend to another. Mrs Diamond rummaged around her shopping basket and produced two chocolate bars and handed one to each of the boys.

"Thanks Mrs Diamond," responded George.

"Cheers Mrs," Billy added.

The two boys tore off the wrappers of the ingredients unknown combination that formed George's favourite snack bar, the Stellar bar!

Mrs Diamond enquired if the bars were a satisfactory treat, "Do you like Stellar bars young man?" aiming her question at her new acquaintance.

Billy responded with a full mouth and grinned through his grunts of pleasure as he munched on his Stellar bar.

When the two boys had finished and thanked Mrs Diamond for their treat they approached the red door of number one Wibble Street. George rapped a knock on the door and waited patiently for someone to answer.

"Knock again, but louder," suggested Billy, who thought George's behaviour a little timid considering that this was his home. They waited some more but still no one came. Billy noted there was no doorbell and suggested he looked through the letterbox to shout. George was adamant that they should wait. Billy couldn't understand his patience. Almost five minutes passed. Billy asked George if he was sure anybody was in and again suggested that he knocked again but louder. Still George insisted they wait and eventually noisy footsteps were heard approaching the door.

Billy thought the steps were awfully heavy sounding for any mother he knew and was wondering how large the woman would be when she eventually answered the door. As the footsteps became louder and louder he was almost convinced it was the walking melody of a hippopotamus or an elephant. 'How large is his mum?' thought Billy. The boys heeded the sound of the lock on the other side of the red door turning and the hinges started to creak open.

Awaiting behind the door to greet the two boys was a hulking towering figure. Billy's eyes fell on the figure's face, unshaven, slightly dirty features, that refused a smile and ushered them in. With a raised thumb that was thrown over its' shoulder in a swift movement. George said nothing and gently moved forward to ease himself by the figure and gestured to Billy to follow him. The two boys disappeared into the kitchen, George searched for his mum. The man who hailed them on their arrival disappeared into the room opposite where the noise of a television could be heard and he quickly disappeared into a room of smoke and closed the door on them.

George found his mum washing pots by the sink.

"Mum, I have my brought my friend to meet you," he whispered.

George's mum paused from her chores and wiped her hands dry on her white apron with red poppy looking flowers dotted around it. She wiped her slightly sweating forehead and patted her short brunette hair as if she was about to meet royalty. She smiled a nervous smile as she welcomed his new playmate. She then queried the time the boys had spent, what had they been up to? Did they meet anyone? The boys politely answered her questions and drank the milk and biscuits she had quickly fetched for them as a welcome for Billy.

"I hope you like it here in Wibble Street. I hope your family like Skaggyness. Where have you moved from?" she asked Billy.

"Well we have lived in lots of places, but we have just come from

Moscow, that's in Russia, miles from here," Billy said proudly.

"Wow, how fascinating! We have always lived here in Skaggyness. I hope you don't get bored here," she said with genuine concern.

"I have lived in lots of places but in all my years I have never lived by the seaside. So, I am really looking forward to messing around down the beach," Billy said with elation.

"There's a lot more in Skaggyness than just the beach front though," insisted George's mum.

"Yes, there's loads of places to investigate and have adventures," chirped George.

"Will George be able to go on treks and ventures with me Mrs Forest? Cos he said he can't leave the street to play," Billy reminded her.

"Well, we'll see," said Mrs Forest.

"Please mum, please, please, please let me go on escapades with Billy," pleaded George.

"Escapades? Where did you learn that word?"

"It's not like we are building a rocket to the moon or anything like that," George argued.

"Although that's not a bad idea," commented Billy.

Billy explained to Mrs Forest how he had a smart mobile phone and that she could have his number. She could ring them whenever she wanted and he would always let her know where they were. George's mother couldn't be anything but impressed with his new friend. Billy appeared to Mrs Forest as a little man who was keen to find his way in this new world. She was almost open-mouthed as Billy relayed some of his adventures he had in other places, even as a five year-old. He boasted he always found his way home and knew danger when he saw it. Billy stated he had a sixth sense and could smell danger. He went into great detail about how his smart phone worked. He explained how he could text her or call her and he could see her on the screen if she also had the right kind of phone.

"I don't have a mobile phone I am afraid Billy, but I think if you let me know where you are both going I think it will be okay," she consented.

"Yes!" the two boys looked at each other excitedly as they scrunched up their fists and waved them in front of their faces as they had just had the green light for a summer of fun.

"You can talk to my mum as well, if you want to," urged Billy.

Mrs Forest said she would and right on cue Billy's mobile phone rang out; it was his father. A quick exchange of pleasantries later the phone was passed for the two mothers to have a chat. The outcomes of the two mothers' conversation was that the boys could head off to the woods, round the corner from them, tomorrow morning while Mrs Forest popped round to see Billy's mum for a coffee and have a 'welcome to Wibble Street' chat.

"That's all settled then boys, you have to go home now Billy, but we'll see you again tomorrow. It was lovely to meet you and I'm looking forward to seeing your mum as well," said Mrs Forest.

"Thanks Mrs Forest, thanks for letting us go to the woods I can't wait to go exploring Skaggyness with George," Billy claimed.

They all moved to the front door and saw Billy out.

"Until the woods!" he shouted as he ran down the street back to number eleven.

George was beaming convinced his summer was going to have far more in it than just playing with the few toys he had alone in his room.

Wobbling Wood

As soon as he had scoffed his breakfast and promised his mother he would keep a sensible head under his red cap George headed for Billy's house. He arrived reddy and willing to do anything with his new pal as they were to investigate the nearby wood.

"You ready?" Billy asked as he greeted him on the step of number eleven Wibble Street.

"Born reddy!" chirped George.

"I guess you were!" Billy replied.

George rambled on to Billy as they headed round the corner of number eleven towards Wobbling Wood. Wobbling Wood, an ordinary wood? Skaggyness doesn't do ordinary!

"Is it a big wood this place?" enquired Billy.

"Dunno, only ever been to the edge and I've never been to any other wood," answered George.

Billy admired him for his honest answers about his life and what he had done with it so far (after all he was only ten years of age). Most boys Billy knew were big heads and boasters, with all that they had done made bigger by their exaggerations and what they hadn't really done was mixed with fantasy. Billy noted carefully how he didn't know George well, yet, but he was sure he wasn't one of his typical knock about pals.

"Have you explored many woods Billy?" asked George. Billy had been to a few woods and forests and had even camped out with his family on more than one occasion.

"Hundreds!" Billy gasped.

"I know you've been to many places and done lots of things," said George with clear admiration for his woody companion.

"There's nothing about woods I don't know. They're dangerous places George. Are you sure you're your brave enough?" he asked.

"I have heard lots of stories about Wobbling Wood but nothing to frighten me," stated George.

"Lions, tigers, snakes, tarantulas...are they in this wood?" inquired Billy with a smirk.

"Don't be silly! This is Wobbling Wood, England, on the edge of Skaggyness! It's not the jungle," George grimaced.

"Pleased to here it!" confirmed Billy.

As they arrived at the edge of Wobbling Wood George paused before venturing forward. Billy stopped with him wondering why he was so apprehensive.

"Why we stopped?"

"I have no idea what's in here," George said with some fear and curiosity. He drew a large breath and then heaved the breath out before drawing two more. The two boys discussed the odour of the wood. George insisted that the wood smelled scary, as Billy laughed and admitted to George that it certainly did have a different whiff

27

than he had ever encountered before from a wood.

George was convinced that the wood should smell of grass and 'naturey' but what he could smell was not that, it was something...? But what he couldn't work out. Billy agreed that the aroma of Wobbling Wood was weird, "I can't place it, the smell that is," Billy agreed.

"We need to go further in," suggested Billy.

"Really? Are you sure? It doesn't smell right, I'm sure of it. So why go further in?" quizzed George.

"We go in BECAUSE it doesn't smell right, which means this wood is more interesting than ever! Come on tomato head!" Billy smiled as he began to creep into the wood. He only went a few steps before turning back to see a quivering red figure rooted to the spot.

"Come on George! What's a matter?" he said with puzzlement.

"Erm, I am not so sure! I think its lunchtime, time to go home!" insisted George.

"It's not long after brekkers mate, we have adventure to find and it smells very, very interesting. Come on? What's wrong frightened of living?" wondered Billy as he challenged George to follow him in. Billy waited for him to move, 'I am not frightened of living,' thought George, 'I'm frightened of not living!' he assured himself.

George walked cautiously towards his companion and when he reached just a few metres inside of the wood where Billy stood eager for his arrival, he leaned against one of the huge oak trees that were the soldiers of the wood, tall, strong with their shoulders back and their chests pushed out waiting for inspection.

As George leaned on the tree this huge Sergeant Major oak creaked over and bent towards the floor like a classroom eraser. George leaped off the tree and it sprang back into place. The two boys just stood and stared at each other. George ran at the tree and he bounced off it and then bounced onto the floor.

"Wicked! A proper rubber tree," Billy shouted in exhilaration. He had a few more 'goes' on the tree while George stood and watched with his gaze transfixed on this amazing tree.

After Billy had used all his breath, George asked him about the other trees. Billy led his companion further into the wood trying all the trees as he went and yes they were all the same. Amazing!

"What a place!" Billy couldn't contain himself.

The two boys had strolled a straight line from the edge of the wood but had wandered some distance with the thrill of their discovery. They sat for a few moments while Billy checked all the trees a few metres back.

"It's okay Redskin Brain I have left marks all on the trees I have bounced on, I can easily find our way back," Billy reassured his pal.

The two boys sat for a while before agreeing that they should start to walk back before they get completely lost, after all it is their first venture into Wobbling Wood, they were sure to come again.

"Look at that!" Billy exclaimed as he pointed at this shed in the middle of the wood just metres from where they sat. No ordinary shed though, this was a golden shed with a golden door. The two boys lifted themselves up and approached this glinting structure dripping with 'alarm signals of danger alerts' for George and 'open my door fun lies here alerts' for Billy. All the windows were solid gold and Billy, in his frustration, banged on the structure angry that he couldn't see inside.

"We have to see inside this!" Billy insisted.

"We don't! We can just imagine and leave at that," suggested George.

"Come on George! I thought you wanted to explore?"

"Help me open this door," Billy asked him as he was forcing the door handle as hard as he could. Being a golden door it was proving very difficult to move. Try as he might Billy couldn't shift the door one way or the other it remained golden and still. Sweat shimmered off Billy's forehead as he took a sharp intake of much needed breath and he watched George stroll over to the door and gently turn the handle of the portal. The golden entrance then simply evaporated right in front of their eyes.

The disappearance of the golden entrance revealed nothing more than darkness, sheer blackness of the blackest kind. There was no light just darkness.

"That's not right?" commented Billy.

"You can't see anything," noted George.

"But its daylight, it doesn't make sense!" Billy continued.

"Why not Billy?" asked George.

"The light from the Sun should shine into the shed, but all we can see is darkness!" Billy said clearly astounded and confused.

"It's just too weird! Let's get out of here," George suggested.

"No fear, we're going in!" stated our blue hero.

"No chance! I'm off!" our not so brave red boy decided.

"Come on!" George tried to drag Billy back in the direction of home, while Billy stood motionless at the point of the floor where the door once stood. George begged him to return home while Billy argued about the thrill of adventure and how the mystery of the Golden Shed of Darkness must be solved. As George argued that there can't be anything in there and as nothing could be seen what would the point be in going in anyway?

Billy argued that maybe it lit up on entering like classroom lights sometimes do. George thought that was a smart idea. George quickly seized on this notion as he wished to try and redeem himself as a courageous boy up for thrills and suddenly decided that he would be first into the house. A bird flew from the hole and a wing brushed passed one of George's ruby cheeks.

"Look at the size of that magpie!" yelped Billy.

"MAGPIE!" panicked George.

"Go on then your royal redness! Off you pop! Into the black!" Billy gestured with his arm outstretched in a 'be my guest' manner and ever so slightly eased George in.

"I will. Watch me!" George said, trying to convince Billy of his bravery. George pulled his red track-suit top down towards his red trackie bottoms and zipped himself-up before taking one large exaggerated stride into the darkness of the Golden Shed.

"Aaaaagggggghhhhh!" was all that could be heard as George disappeared into the confident dimness in front of them.

The surprised screaming was followed by a firm thud!

"Are you alright?" enquired Billy.

George was in sheer fright and not without pain, his ankle was twisted and he ached all over, but he was determined not to let Billy know how he was suffering.

"Yeh, I am just fine!" exclaimed George.

George could see nothing but the blackness, it was blacker than he ever imagined black could be, not even a chink of light anywhere he moved his peepers. What was also strange was that he could hear Billy's voice as if he was right next to him, and 'something else' thought George. He paused to try and work out what else it was that was so strange about the situation. 'Smell!' thought George, 'this place

31

smells of nothing! I can't smell anything!'

"Can you climb out?" shouted Billy down to him.

"I can't see anything and I can't feel anything," he replied.

Thinking frantically Billy pondered how he was going to help George, after all he had no real idea of how far down George was or if he had the tools he needed, such as a rope, to lift George back up to him.

Billy was suddenly startled as a huge paw suddenly appeared on his right shoulder, placing mud on his blue top. His eyes bulged to the size of saucers as he froze in fear of what he was about to turn and face. Billy's body tightened as every muscle became tight and panic crept up his body. 'What on earth?' Billy's mind was running riot, looking sideways at this claw type furry thing that had landed on his being.

The Golden Abyss

"Everything okay up there?" George shouted as he lay in pain and frustration as he was desperate for Billy to solve his predicament. Billy had his own quandary and didn't answer George for fear of startling the creature attached to him. George was now in utter panic as he couldn't hear his new friend's voice and inside began to cry fearing he was doomed.

A voice whispered in Billy's ear.

"Can we be of any assistance?" the voice asked.

Amazed, Billy spun round to come face-to-face with the face of a squirrel, all grey with white fur around his nose and mouth, a squirrel the same size as him, well a little larger actually, kind of Dad sized!

Billy was speechless as he blinked and pinched himself convinced he was dreaming. He looked the giant squirrel up and down only to notice that he had teeth like a rabbit and two big floppy black ears, odd! He had a long bushy grey tail, as a squirrel should.

Nervously, Billy inquired to the 'thing', in search for some kind of animal identity, "Wwwhat are you?"

"We are the Squibbits!" the furry animal responded, in a very warm and kind voice.

Billy began to ease his tension and as he looked all around him as an army of squibbits peered at him poking their heads from around the trees they were hiding behind. 'Wow' Billy thought as these creatures cautiously hopped towards him.

"We can help you," the talking Squibbit said reassuringly to Billy.

"How can you guys help?" queried the blue one.

"Your friend's down in the deep isn't he?"

"Yes. Have you been watching us?"

"Yes, very carefully. We have to protect ourselves first but we are peaceful creatures and do not like to see suffering and distress. The Golden Shed has fooled many who believe there are riches inside but all that glitters is not great gold!" the talking squibbit affirmed.

The squibbit continued, "Your friend will not be the first we have rescued from the abyss!"

"Really? What is the shed all about? Why is it golden?" Billy tried to gain as much information as possible; as was always his way.

"It's a mystery. Many believe it is a gateway to another world, some think it is a graveyard for the greedy and others believe there is treasure and riches beyond belief sunk deep into the blackness. But no one has survived long enough down there to either see or find anything," the squibbit explained.

"You can help my friend?" Billy's voice went higher as his concern for George returned post haste as George was heard shouting for help from below.

"Yes, please leave it to us we will get him out! I promise."

"I am Razor and these are my team of squibbits here to your friend

George's rescue,"

"You know his name?"

Hurriedly, Razor stated, "We have big ears to catch almost all of the sounds of the wood. We have watched and listened to you both Billy. Now let us get to work." Billy moved quickly to the edge of the Golden Shed and shouted down that everything up above had gone quite mad but he would soon be rescued. George was relieved to hear Billy's voice again. Razor gathered the other squibbits in a huddle like a top- football team just before kick-off, their paws spreading dirt all over their grey fur. The team of rescue squibbits proceeded to listen intently to their leader as he shared his plan.

Razor quickly turned to Billy, as they broke their huddle, and shared the plan explaining what they were going to do. Billy relayed the idea down to George.

"You are to curl up in a ball and don't be frightened," he shouted down to his quivering pal.

Responding quickly, "Good plan!" George retorted.

Pausing for a moment, George responded with a concerning voice, "Why?"

"Erm..." Billy thought carefully about what he was to utter next as even he couldn't believe the craziness of his words.

"A giant nut is going come down to you and another giant nut will soon follow," Billy said struggling to trust his own statement.

"Oh! Is that all!" hollered George.

"As the nuts come down, you are to climb on them and brace yourself for the next one falling. Eventually you will be able to climb all the way to the top," Billy said sharing the rescue plan with the rescuee.

"Makes sense!" replied George scratching his head, 'Giant nuts! What's he on? He'll be telling me there's giant squirrels up there' mumbled George to himself.

By now, Razor had organised his team into one long squibbit chain stretching from the biggest tree in Wobbling Wood all the way to the edge of the Golden Shed. Billy watched mesmerised as the squibbits passed one giant nut from squibbit to squibbit eventually reaching the front of the chain where Razor was waiting to usher the nut down for George to climb onto.

Billy stood behind Razor at the portal of the Golden Shed and bellowed down to George as Razor as he was about to send the first nut hurtling down to his lost buddy.

"Brace yourself! Nuts away!" Billy warned George.

George was curled up as tight as he could, just as he had been instructed to do, he held on to the thought that he would soon see the light again. During all the time he had been down there his eyes had not adjusted, it was as black now as it was when he was first introduced to the base of the Golden Abyss, as this hole had now become to both Billy and George.

'Ow' he thought as the first nut bounced off him, he felt his way around the nut and climbed on top. The second nut soon arrived and lodged itself in the space that was available next to the first. The hole appeared narrower than George had first imagined and he climbed a little higher onto the following nut. Before long nuts were flowing into the abyss and as George fumbled and climbed higher and higher the pain in his ankle went slowly away, as did all the pain in his body.

Eventually, two hands emerged gripping the top of the hole where the Golden Door to the Golden Shed had once been. One arm tucked into a blue sleeve grabbed George's right arm and two furry paws gripped his left. The red super hero was then lifted back into the light. George quickly placed his arm over his eyes as he was momentarily blinded by his return to the light of the day.

Billy stood there scratching his head and was prompted to ask the rescued party, "Are you okay mate?"

"Never better," George had a huge smile all over his face, all his pain had gone, he had no hunger, no thirst and didn't feel at all tired.

"Look at the state of you now!" exclaimed Billy, "How will you explain that to your mum?"

"What do you mean? I'm fine," George restated.

Positively trembling with excitement, "I can see that, you are cleaner now than when you went in! Did you have a bath down there?" Billy quizzed.

Brashly George claimed, "No, I am just dead hard! I wasn't frightened, even for a second," he insisted, determined to impress his blue pal.

"You had mud on your knees and an egg stain on your t-shirt and your hair was a bit dirty when you fell in, now you're spotless! Explain that!" demanded Billy.

Razor and the squibbits did not stay or utter another word, they simply faded back into the wood in the same manner they appeared. As George's sight fully adjusted back to the light Billy suggested George should thank Razor for his rescue. As he turned towards Razor to introduce his friend he suddenly realised Razor was no longer in the vicinity and neither were any of the fantastic squibbit rescue team.

"Who's Razor?" asked George.

"Well, he is ... half..." Billy paused and stopped himself, not really believing his own eyes and ears.

"It doesn't matter," Billy insisted, thinking that George just wouldn't believe him.

Billy then passed the whole rescue off by explaining that he was helped by a passing man and woman who were just walking their dog who just happened to know where there was a stash of giant nuts that were regularly used to rescue fallen children in that specific hole.

George didn't press the issue, but as they walked back towards the edge of Wobbling Wood and Wibble Street it was Billy who was slow, dirty looking and tired but George had energy to burn. George was to be heard above the all sounds of the wood elated to be out of the Golden Abyss. He bounced along the trees all the way to the edge of the wood heading back towards home with a clear and definite idea of the right direction. Meanwhile, Billy dragged himself silently behind him somewhat tired and oh so very confused.

"Up for another adventure tomorrow?" George asked enthusiastically.

The day's events had just been too much for Billy to absorb and he thought about lying on his bed trying to make sense of it all. He wondered if he should try to tell anyone about what he had witnessed in the wood, 'I'll start a diary', he thought. He decided he wouldn't share it with anyone, after all he wasn't sure if even he believed all of what he had witnessed.

Persistently, George asked again, "Up for something again tomorrow?" as Billy returned to the moment and addressed his companion's question.

"Erm...can we just a kick a ball in the street mate, a bit of footie, I think I need a calmer few days, George"

"Okay, can if you like," George agreed just pleased to feel great and have a friend to share adventures and scrapes.

They walked silently all the way to Wibble Street with Billy still trying to get his head round the events of Wobbling Wood. As they reached number eleven, Billy yawned and gave George a lazy thumbs-up.

George was still full of boundless energy, almost bouncing along the street.

Utterly joyous, George shouted down the street, "Welcome to Skaggyness!" as he sprinted, with a big grin on his face, down to number one.

Ancient Diamond

It was mid-morning on another sunny school holiday Wednesday, Billy and George were passing a brand new pink and black leather cased football to each other in the street. The side of number one Wibble Street proved itself useful as the two boys were engaging in a game of walley. Billy seemed to have the beating of George and started to show–off his keepy-uppy skills and then challenged George to beat his total. George was counting, fifty-one, fifty-two (he switched from his right-foot to his left-foot and then onto his knees) fifty-three, fifty-four. Billy then nudged the ball to George to start his turn…one, two, three…"Here you are."

George couldn't get beyond three but was quite happy watching Billy show-off his fine close control of a football. "This is how it's done tomato head!" They were interrupted by Mrs Diamond emerging from number two. It was a warm day and Billy thought it strange that this old lady should be wearing a black leather motorcycle jacket and black leather gloves. Billy paused to turn to George and asked him if she had a motorbike, George replied in the negative that she definitely did not have a motorcycle!

"Good morning boys!" she called out as she approached them in the street, with her shopping basket trailing behind her.

"Morning Mrs Diamond," George replied.

"Are you biking Mrs?" Billy asked her.

"No young man, just toddling to the shops," she politely explained.

It still seemed strange to Billy that an old woman should wear such attire to go to the shops and he sensed something was amiss in this act, after all it was such a warm fine day with zero wind and cloud.

A huge magpie was perched high on the wall watching the boys; Billy nudged George and suggested that the bird might be Mickey Magpie escaped from police custody.

"Don't joke about something like that, he might come back here looking for trouble," suggested George with genuine fear.

Mrs. Diamond chirped, "He's only half-joking, Mickey Magpie escaped yesterday after the police let him go to the toilet just before he appeared in court."

Billy continued the story for her, "Yes apparently, he was in cuffs and in the fourth floor gents lavvy. After a while he didn't come out so they went in after him."

Mrs. Diamond was determined to finish the story, "YES young man and all they found when they burst in there was the cuffs on the floor, an open window and two feathers – one black and one white."

George went quite pale. Billy suggested to Mrs. Diamond that it was rather warm for a leather jacket.

She continued to explain herself, "Us older folk feel the wind you know!"

"Be good now and I might treat you to a Stellar Bar when I get back, if you mind you don't kick the ball into me flowers!" she gestured towards her uniformed red, yellow and white flowers that adorned the front of her home.

The boys knew that she would be true to her word. They gave her a promising nod and both lads shared a grin with her at the prospect of a gift of another delicious Stellar bar.

41

As Mrs Diamond shuffled round the corner, heading for the shops, Billy pondered.

"Where does she get those Stellar bars?" Billy enquired to his companion.

"No idea! My mum has looked all over Skaggyness but she has never come across them," George replied.

"My mum did ask her once but she simply smiled and told her she snatched them from when she passed the stars in space!" continued George.

Billy laughed and thought this was just yet another mystery of Skaggyness that needed an explanation. Billy persuaded George to put the football aside so that they could follow Mrs Diamond to the shops and find these gorgeous Stellar bars that tasted 'out of this world'. They cautiously approached the corner of Wibble Street and grabbed hold of the edge of the extended wall from number one. They poked their heads around the wall and spied Mrs Diamond shuffling along.

This was a strange street they were looking at; on one side there was the Skaggyness wall (eight metres high and four metres thick, made of battleship grey granite stone) which surrounded the town like a prison or a castle; the other side, another wall some twelve metres high of the same stone with a wide pavement on either side carpeted with jet black tarmac and one long white painted stripe down the centre of the road.

This street was Twilight Street, but no-one lived here and there was nothing in it but granite, tarmac and concrete. Twilight Street was never blessed with sunlight a spot in the world never out of shadow.

Billy's eyes never left Mrs Diamond and was quick to remind George they must keep their distance as they didn't want to give the game away to her.

"I need to tie me laces," George informed his pal and bent down to address the lace issue on both feet.

"Hurry-up," Billy urged.

Billy's eyes never left Mrs Diamond but he couldn't fathom what he was seeing. He watched open mouthed as she manoeuvred herself and her shopping trolley into the middle of the road, no vehicles in sight, she leant into her shopping basket and with two hands produced a shiny scarlet crash helmet.

She quickly placed the helmet on her head, adjusted the chin strap, pulled down a metal strap from the bag of the basket, stepped onto it and pressed a big shiny red button on the handle of her basket. While George was still tying the laces on his training shoes, Billy stared frozen as when the big red button was pressed it ignited a powerful, but strangely quiet, rocket from the bottom of the shopping basket and it propelled her speedily towards the sky. In the blink-of-an-eye she shot over the wall and across the clouds, disappearing from Billy's view in less than a minute.

"You missed it! You flippin' missed it you great radish head!" Billy gasped as George appeared, unaware of her impressive exit from the street, at his side. 'Makes a change from tomato head, I guess' thought George.

"Missed what?" George responded somewhat bemused.

"Mrs Diamond's just blasted off towards space!" exclaimed Billy.

"Of course she has, I believe you!" George stood there looking at his friend shaking his head.

"She's about three thousand years-old, I don't flippin' think so!" disputed George.

Billy quickly realised that the idea was rather fanciful, unless you saw it with your own eyes.

"Have it your way then! Either way, we have lost her!" claimed Billy.

"I am sure she is doing NOTHING exciting anyway," asserted George.

"Errm," muttered Billy as he said nothing more about what he witnessed the kind old lady do.

Meanwhile, Mrs Diamond was hurtling to who knows where? After just a few minutes of blasting through the sky, breaking out from the Earth's atmosphere into space and then re-entering the land of oxygen, her shopping basket was propelling her somewhere…but where?

She reached for the big red button once again and pressed it firmly – twice- as she was moving at the speed of a missile towards the ground. The basket grew a parachute and quickly stalled to a float as the Earth's floor came into view and the rocket's engine fell silent. Mrs Diamond then began to ease safely down towards the ground.

A young man soon appeared by her side with feathered wings. Mrs Diamond was taken aback to see such a handsome young man, muscle bound, with olive toned skin. The youth appeared next to her in the middle of the sun kissed sky. She noted that the flying man had his wings made from feathers and wax.

Proudly he announced himself, "I am Icarus!" with his wings in fully controlled hover mode.

"So you must be!" Mrs Diamond replied.

"I am Mrs Diamond!" and the gentle descent continued as did their conversation.

"You are a strange woman. I wonder why you're being here, near to this great land of ours? Are you some sort of trick gift from the Trojans or maybe you are from Sparta?" the boy persisted to establish a truth that would satisfy himself and his people, after all he must know was she a friend or a foe?

"I know who you are," Mrs Diamond insisted.

"You are Icarus, son of the master craftsman Daedalus, who made those fancy wings upon your person from nothing more than feathers and wax," she proudly displayed her knowledge of the myths and legends of Ancient Greece.

"I will talk with you more when we land young man," Mrs Diamond had no fear as her basket landed gently to the ground.

Icarus had floated down with her and they had landed just outside a city that was basking in searing heat which had Mrs Diamond tearing off her jacket, helmet and gloves as fast she could. Icarus brought her water from a well close by. When watered and air restored into her body she packed her equipment away in her basket and she asked Icarus to show her around; he gleefully consented.

"Ancient Greece! How exciting!" enthused Mrs Diamond.

"Show me everything! Although, I only have a day!" cackled Mrs Diamond.

Mrs Diamond and Icarus strolled (not shuffled) around the city of Athens, as Icarus enthused over showing this stranger from another land around his home and his people, with her basket trailing behind her. Icarus explained how the city of Athens was the most important city of ancient Greece, and the main centre for all forms of learning and arts.

Icarus pointed to a grand building high on a hill.

"Look there! That is the Acropolis! There you will find the Parthenon, a temple dedicated to the goddess Athena!" Icarus was clearly so proud of this grand building.

"Errm, Athena, the goddess of wisdom and warfare," stated Mrs

Diamond.

"You know so much already," noted Icarus.

Athens is named after the goddess Athena and Icarus gestured for Mrs Diamond to sit down so that they could talk more and take a drink. They sat on a stone bench round the agora (an open space for meeting and trading activity). They talked for an hour and a little more about the troubles of Athens and the stories that they both had about the gods of Ancient Greece, the wars Athens faced and the wars still to come.

"Beware young Icarus, the Persians will come, you must look to Perikles!" she confidently informed Icarus.

"You are a curious woman but I feel that you are a fountain of wisdom and knowledge, a little like Athena!" Icarus marked her words.

"What is your land like?" Icarus asked of Mrs Diamond.

"Well, the weather's not as grand as it is here me duck. We have learned much from Greece," she informed her inquisitor.

Mrs Diamond then explained how in her homeland the country is run by 'democracy'. She told him of the Palace of Westminster where many governments have been strongly influenced by the democratic system which developed in Athens. The Greek word 'democracy' means 'power of the people'.

Icarus started to argue with her.

"It is true, the meaning of democracy is as you say but right now in Greece the great 'power of the people' that you talk about does not exist. No women, foreigners or slaves can vote. Only working Greek men, rich men and soldiers have 'democracy' in Greece today!" Icarus declared.

"It will change!" asserted Mrs Diamond.

"If you say so!" Icarus agreed not wanting to fall out with his new companion.

Icarus wanted to take Mrs Diamond home to meet his father, the famous Daedalus – the master craftsman and enjoy Greek hospitality with a meal with his family. He explained how his father had been away at another home of theirs in Crete, working on a secret project for King Minos, but he would return this very evening.

Mrs Diamond had a quick glance at her wrist watch and quickly hid it back under her light blue blouse sleeve not wanting to have to explain such an advanced time piece to Icarus while he still judged time by the Sun. She accepted his invitation to dine with joy and was looking forward to the Greek feast she had been promised. Icarus explained that only very good friends have ever been to their home and that the Greeks liked their homes to be places of family privacy.

As the sun began to set, Mrs Diamond and Icarus arrived at his family home somewhat hungry and very thirsty. Daedalus was not around, but his mother beckoned her in and after a few exchanges of words and greetings, his mother pulled Icarus aside. She asked him if Mrs Diamond was a crazy lady that he had brought home just to annoy her.

"No! She is fascinating and wise! Trust me and trust her!" insisted Icarus.

Goodbye To Icarus

Mrs Diamond took close note of the Ancient Greek home she had been made warmly welcome in. The windows were small and set high on the walls which were made out of sun-dried mud bricks. Mrs Diamond couldn't help thinking that 'this house won't last long!' She noted the slave through in another room who was busy washing pots.

In the porch she had noted a statue; she asked Icarus who the statue was of.

"This is Hermes! He is a son of Zeus and he is a helpful God, a creating God!" Icarus insisted that she took it home and he placed it in her basket. Mrs Diamond was delighted with the gift but was at first reluctant to accept until Icarus showed her that there was a statue of Hermes in nearly every room of the house.

Icarus invited Mrs Diamond to learn a few games that the Greeks played while his mother prepared a meal. He explained to her about how rich Greeks, especially those who lived in towns, had plenty of leisure time to spend talking, giving dinner parties, visiting the gymnasium, and playing all kinds of games.

He showed her some of the musical instruments around the house; stringed instruments like the harp, the lyre, and the kithara (a kind of lyre), and wind instruments like the syrinx, or pan pipes, made of reeds of different sizes. Mrs Diamond cheekily asked if she could dance with him making the most of the attention from such a handsome young chap. Icarus politely explained that Greek men did many things; hunt, make, fight, create new things, think deeply about all issues of life but they definitely don't dance, he insisted that in Ancient Greece only women dance!

As the evening wore on Icarus and Mrs Diamond shared water and grapes while they waited for the feast that was being prepared. Icarus taught her how to play 'Knucklebones'. 'Knucklebones' he explained, was a woman's game and the 'Knucklebones' were made from the ankle-joints of small, cloven-footed animals. He explained how to play 'Kottabos'. Mrs Diamond loved this game as she had to hold a wine cup by one handle and then flick the dregs of wine from the cup at a target. Icarus beat her as he hit the target, a shield on the wall, most accurately.

"What a hoot!" exclaimed Mrs Diamond.

They settled down by playing a game that appeared to Mrs Diamond as to be similar to 'Snakes and Ladders'. Mrs Diamond was having a brilliant time!

The two of them shared stories about sports and both exchanged tales about the Olympic Games. Icarus excitedly told her about sports and how the Greeks used sports to train for war. He told her all about the Olympic Games being held every four years at Olympia to honour the chief god of the Greeks, Zeus.

Mrs Diamond said that the Greek Olympics would bring many countries together in the future. The festival would bring together lands and people from around the world to compete in the very sports that were practised that same day in Athens. Icarus proudly told her how he competed in the discus, long jump and spear throw.

As Icarus's father returned home, Daedalus – the master craftsman, was not sure about the presence of Mrs Diamond in the family home.

Daedalus beckoned Icarus to come to him for a quiet word. Daedalus asked his son whether she was a 'crazy lady?', but Icarus insisted she was wise and kind. Daedalus kept his manners as his wife gestured for Mrs Diamond and Icarus to sit in the andron (dining room).

"Mrs Diamond, welcome to my home!" Daedalus suddenly announced in a booming manner and he ushered Mrs Diamond to her seat at the table. She was placed opposite Icarus with his father and his mother at either end of the banqueting stone table. Slave girls served the wine as all four drank merrily and discussed the state of Athens and the problems the country had. Mrs Diamond was having a wonderful time with a smile fixed upon her face. When she returned home she knew she wouldn't ever tell a living soul of this adventure; after all...who would believe her?

The table soon filled with other guests and family as almost twenty sat around the table and exchanged stories and sang hymns to the gods.

Daedalus suddenly banged a hammer on the stone table and told his guests he had an announcement to make. All the guests went quiet and waited for Daedalus' next words.

He began, "Today I have returned from Crete after planning a great feat of Greek brilliance."

Daedalus continued after a quick swig of wine.

"For the great King Minos, I have been asked to construct a Labyrinth. It will be an underground maze of paths and chambers. The Labyrinth will lie close to his place at Knossos," he boasted.

He took a further glug of liquid before continuing, "The Labyrinth will be a prison for the famous Minotaur, the half-man, half-bull like creature of Crete!"

"I am to be paid handsomely for my work and I was even sent away with a gentle kiss on my cheek from the beautiful daughter of King Minos, Ariadne. I can share with you that Princess Ariadne is as heavenly in her deed as she is in her face!"

Daedalus finished his speech and slumped back into his chair with a further slush of his wine. His guests roared their approval and burst into delightful cheers.

The guests all wore garlands and perfume. Mrs Diamond noted the beautiful mix of smell. The conversation flowed from politics and philosophy, but as they drank more and more wine, they told each other jokes, riddles and stories of time now gone.

The food accompanied the wine and conversation. Mrs Diamond tucked into bread and goat's cheese (from the family goat), olives were available all evening with bread plentiful. She enjoyed a great feast of lentils, peas, onions, garlic and cabbage. She tucked into fish and different cheeses. She gorged on pomegranates, figs, apples and pears. She had a little bit of all sorts of things; she had a plate full of fish: some sturgeon, mullet, mackerel and tuna.

Mrs Diamond urged Icarus to tell a joke.

Obligingly he began, "Wishing to teach his donkey not to eat, his master did not offer him any food. When the donkey died of hunger, he said: - I've had a great loss. Just when he had learned not to eat...he died!" Icarus roared with laughter at his own joke, but Mrs Diamond could only manage a polite smile.

Mrs Diamond tried a joke of her own, "What is the most popular children's film in Ancient Greece?"

"I do not understand! What is film?" interrupted Icarus.

"Troy story!" laughed Mrs Diamond, clearly pleased with her own jovial attempt.

After forcing down a small squid, Mrs Diamond snatched a quick look at the time and hastily leaned into Icarus and whispered that she must leave. Icarus held her arm for a second and assured her that they would slip quietly away.

Mrs Diamond and Icarus strolled back to the place they had landed earlier that day. This place was a whole kilometre out of the view of the hustle and bustle of Athens on a summer evening. Icarus spoke of his delight of the entertainment of the day and Mrs Diamond also.

"You must come back one day!" Icarus begged of her.

"Maybe!" Mrs Diamond smiled at him and double checked she still had the statue of Hermes in her basket, a tourist's souvenir. She had dragged that basket everywhere with her, all day.

Mrs Diamond dressed herself back into her leather jacket, her gloves and helmet. She stepped back onto the metal step and prepared for take-off.

Totally overwhelmed, "I will fly with you as far as I can," insisted Icarus.

"You won't be able to keep up young man!" boasted Mrs Diamond.

"I try! Surely I will be faster, I am so much younger!" argued Icarus.

Icarus started to flap his wings he had once again equipped himself with on his person and lifted himself a metre from the ground hovering while still chatting to Mrs Diamond.

"Promise me one thing young Icarus!" asked Mrs Diamond.

"I don't make promises!" insisted Icarus.

"Take my advice then! Don't fly too high; don't fly too close to the Sun! It will be your end!" promised the silver haired friend of the young Icarus. She reached out and put one hand on his shoulder, a silent thankyou and farewell. In a moment Mrs Diamond pressed her ignition button and like a bolt of lightning she catapulted high into the sky back up amongst the stars. Icarus was stunned how fast she disappeared from his gaze. He whispered to himself, "What have I met today? Did a god reveal itself to me?"

As she passed through the stars she reached out and grabbed hand sized Stellar Bars that were aimlessly floating about, after all Mrs Diamond did promise the children one each on her return.

She landed back in the very spot that she had left in Twilight Street, earlier that day. She quickly tucked the parachute into the basket and placed the helmet on the huge pile of silk. She dusted herself down and was sure no one had seen her, strangely there never seemed to be people or transport using Twilight Street very much. She shuffled back towards Wibble Street and as she turned the corner she met her young friends George and Billy.

"Did you get all you needed from the SHOPS!?" enquired Billy somewhat rudely and to George's surprise.

"Oh, I think so, thanks for asking," said Mrs Diamond as they both gave each other an uneasy angry glare.

Mrs Diamond checked her flowers were still intact and thanked the boys for not doing them any damage. She reached inside her basket and rummaged around searching for something. She took a few moments with both boys looking at her in anticipation and sure enough their hopes were matched well with the production of two Stellar bars. Mrs Diamond handed them to the boys as she quickly shuffled off to number two quickly disappearing through the door without saying another word.

The two boys opened the wrappers of their Stellar bars and pulled a face of despair as they were greeted by two melted bars of what appears to them to be sparkling chocolate and caramel.

"Shall we put them in the fridge for a bit?" suggested George.

"No, let's just scoff 'em" Billy retorted as he was shoving the biscuit based bar down his throat and wearing the sparkling chocolate and caramel on his face.

The Wall

It was a slightly overcast day with the dampness of the ground freshly sprinkled all around and Billy was eager to explore. He appeared at George's door knocking ferociously. George's mum greeted Billy with her customary smile that seemed to captivate him every time. Billy could never resist smiling back at her.

"Morning Billy! You're early…he's just finishing his breakfast!" she explained.

Billy was keen, while he had lay wide awake in the middle of the night he had decided that he and Billy would be exploring the mysterious wall that surrounded Skaggyness. He thought about the events of Wobbling Wood and how he had watched Mrs. Diamond disappear high into the sky and on to who knows where. He decided that the wall was going to show him something special today and he was keen to share this adventure with his only friend so far in Skaggyness. George appeared by his mum's side and said nothing as he tuned into Billy and his mum's conversation. Breadcrumbs continually dropped onto George's scarlet sweatshirt as he was finishing-off his toast.

Billy started to lay out the days' agenda to them both as he described his plan for the two boys to cycle around the perimeter of the inside wall of Skaggyness. Mrs. Forest stopped him in all his exciting chatter and pointed out that there was just a little problem in the fact that George didn't have a bike. Billy said he had the answer to that problem and asked his red pal if he was up for the adventure if he could get him a bike. George responded with an emphatic yes by yelping that he was 'well-up' for it!

Billy quickly sprinted home and within minutes was knocking again on the scarlet door of number one. George and his ma greeted the blue lad from number eleven once again; they both stood in the door way open-mouthed staring at a beaming Billy who was equipped with blue cycling gloves and a blue safety helmet and sat astride a gleaming blue racing bike. On Billy's right hand-side he was clutching a petite bright pink bike ever so slightly smaller (quite a bit smaller really) framed bike complete with red, white and blue tassels on the either side of the handle bars.

"It's my sister's!" Billy announced proudly as the two jaw-dropped residents of number one couldn't have worked out for themselves.

"There's a little basket at the front look, in case we find something interesting," Billy continued to beam eager to get the adventure underway.

George creaked his head slowly round and stared in disbelief at his mother, he lingered for a few seconds with a look of desperation on his face and gently creaked back his glare at the pink vehicle his friend had brought for him to use. Billy held out his arm straight with a pink helmet that had some yellow flowers dotted all around it. Billy explained that you cannot ride a bike without a helmet so George would have to wear it.

Mrs. Forest had to put her hand over her mouth to stop herself from bursting into laughter as she watched her gorgeous George cautiously take the helmet from the outstretched hand that was enthusiastically thrusting it forward. George ever so gently slipped the helmet on and silently strapped it under his chin, mounted the bike and took one more desperate look at his giggling mother as George led out the two boy convoy.

The two of them rode steadily round the corner into Twilight Street where Billy was becoming more and more convinced that the street looked like an airport runway with walls. He was much more confident about cycling than George and was increasingly edging away from his panting cycling partner.

Billy was looking over his shoulder shouting encouragingly, "Come on George! Get your legs moving!"

George did try to get his little legs to move faster but his bike seemed to go the same speed however rapid he pedalled. Twilight Street was deserted as usual but as they neared the end to turn towards Skaggyness centre the sun hit their faces and they paused for breath.

As they gazed down the road they could see the sea that lapped the edge of Skaggyness. George suggested that they headed for the beach but Billy had other plans. The blue boy was determined to find a gap in the wall so he knew how to exit and enter into the town; for wherever he went in Skaggyness so far he had felt hemmed in by a huge, unscalable wall.

Billy then spotted the brand new hypermarket that had only opened a few days before.

As quick as a flash he asked, "Have you got any cash on you?"

"I've got a quid, but that's just in case I have to phone home in an emergency," George answered.

"I've got my mobile here so you could spend that pound in the shop. (Looking over at the hypermarket.) It's absolutely huge, look at it, it goes on forever!" yarned Billy. He was determined to pop his head through the doors and take a peek.

The two cycled towards an entrance to the shop and parked their bikes. "You'll have to stay with the bikes while I look around," Billy instructed.

They didn't have a bike lock so George was left holding the two cycles as his blue adorned pal went in to the new superstore that he had heard all the parents raving about. George meanwhile was left reading a poster:

Welcome to The Olympic Super Store!

Citius, Altius, Fortius!

Our customer promise is to get you served faster!

Keep the choice of items higher!

Keep your pound stronger!

Billy emerged some minutes later from the shop clutching two ice-creams in cones. He handed George his which was just a simple whipped ice cream and tucked in merrily to his own which was the same as George's but twice as much as ice cream with a stick of chocolate sticking out of it, the top of the ice cream was adorned with hundreds and thousands and raspberry juice. Billy's monster ice cream made George's look pathetic.

"Mine was a bit more than a pound, if you were wondering," Billy informed his pal.

Billy observed, "It's like a huge adventure playground in the Olympic (super store). I nearly got lost just looking for the ice-creams. We'll have to come back another time. You need a day or maybe two!"

With the ice-cream vanquished, they continued to follow the outside of the wall and soon enough, on passing the end of the hypermarket a clear gap in the wall emerged. Billy paused to breathe and watched the wall's entrance intently. He said nothing to George as the red one pulled his bike alongside him. Billy sat pausing for thought, anticipating that something would pass through the break in the wall that formed a way out of Skaggyness. They both watched in stillness, Billy looking for something different as to what you might expect and with George just staring, sensing he should just follow his chum.

Minutes passed and not one solitary car, bike, man, woman, child or dog came through in or out of the access area. 'Strange!' thought Billy to himself, but strange is what Billy had come to expect from his short time in Skaggyness.

"Let's go through the exit and out of Skaggyness," he suggested to his companion.

George protested, "I can't do that my Dad will kill me! I am not allowed to beyond the wall."

Billy was not going to take no for an answer.

"Your dad is never going to know!"

Nervously, "If he even thinks I've gone outside the wall, he'll go ballistic!" George insisted.

Billy sensed real fear from his red buddy, especially about his father.

"All we're going to do is cycle to the other side of that wall, then turn the bikes round and come back to this very spot!" George persisted.

George continued to remonstrate, "You don't understand Billy. Nobody in our family has ever been out of Skaggyness! I don't think we're allowed."

"Not allowed! What kind of utter tosh is that?" Billy bellowed clearly angry at what he considered to be rubbish thinking.

"Well I'm going through and so are you."

George was now physically shaking with fear, it hadn't taken Billy very many days to develop a strong pull on him. George was not keen to displease his companion so he decided to do what he requested, after all they would come straight back. He wanted to be more like Billy, somebody he saw as tough and adventurous. George watched on nervously as Billy started to pedal towards the two edges of the wall at the town's exit.

Billy had sensed, some days ago, that the wall was going to be something special and now he suspected he was going to find out what that special property was. He had hoped that by going through the exit it would be a time portal or some other manner of super transport to a magical time or place.

Billy had dragged his beautiful blue bike to the side of the street giving him a twenty metre approach so that he could gather-up some speed. George, still shaking and now sweating looked on.

Billy glanced at his bike and then focused his gaze on the road exiting the wall. There was no sign of traffic and so he started his advance. As he got closer, he pedalled faster and faster and George had a sharp intake of breath. Billy was on the other side now, he looked all around him it was just road, fields and a signpost to the M1 motorway. What a disappointment! Billy quickly turned his attention to George.

The thunder had been exactly that, thunder! The clouds had been gathering above them and the sky had grown dark.

Insistently, "Your turn George! Come on! There's nothing to worry about." Billy reassured his friend.

"Okay! I'm coming!" replied our red super hero. 'Super powers, don't fail me now," George told himself.

As George could clearly see a smiling Billy on the other side of the wall, he feared slightly less the consequences he might face by breaching the divide. He had only his father's order not to breach the wall to sweat on. He copied Billy's style and took a twenty metre retreat before pedalling as fast he could towards his comrade.

As George got within five metres of the wall's exit a huge magpie swooped down and flew right in front of his eyes. As Billy passed through the divide in the wall a seemingly large clap of thunder struck; a bolt of lightning lit up the sky and the heaven's opened as it poured the heaviest of rains that were to bounce all along the roads and pavements. As George came in line with the wall he was swiftly removed from his bike by a seemingly invisible force and was rapidly put on his rear while the bike gently rolled straight to the open stretched hand of the awaiting Billy. Momentarily, Billy watched and shook his head.

"Get up George and walk towards me!"

"I can't. I can't get passed the wall. I told you we are not allowed," George asserted.

"You jumped off the bike! Why? You can't be that scared of your dad! Surely!"

George repeated his assertion, "We aren't allowed outside of the wall. We can't get through the space and that flamin' great magpie put me off!"

Billy brought the bikes to where his mate was now sat on the road with rain bouncing off both of them. Both were now slowly getting soaked. As George got to his feet, somewhat dejected and confused, Billy quickly grabbed him and desperately tried to pull him through the exit. He pulled and pulled and pulled with every muscle he could find but still George could not or would not move. His body merely leaned towards Billy while his feet were as if they had been nailed to the road. Billy eventually became cold with the rain and weak from trying. He picked up his bike and thrust his sister's cycle towards a rain soaked George.

"Now do you believe me? I...cannot...leave ... Skaggyness! And don't ask me why because I don't know!" he smiled as for once he felt that he had been right and Billy had been proved wrong. They both headed for the bus shelter near the Olympic Super Store. In the bus shelter they both shivered and watched as a bus approached. It was the number 26 bus to Beston.

"Where's Beston?" Billy asked.

"Dunno. Never been. Not allowed out of Skaggyness!" replied a dripping cold and now miserable George.

"Yeh…you said," Billy was already plotting alternative ways of one day getting George out of Skaggyness. Billy was a born adventurer and yearned for his pal to see the world like he had. They were both now soaked to the skin and the red one and the blue one remounted their bikes to head home. Billy glanced once more at the wall and the exit. As his look lingered he watched the number 26 to Beston go through the exit unimpeded. As the bus passed through on either side of the battleship grey granite stone wall, it seemed the wall was wearing a smile on both sides of the divide. The two boys cycled back from whence they came, bedraggled and bemused.

Mr. Horn And The Ghosts

As George and Billy cycled back to drop-off their bikes, both dishevelled, dirty, wet and cold as the rain relentlessly threw itself at the ground. George shouted, "Ay up Mr. Horn!" and waved at the man entering number three Wibble Street.

"Is that the teacher you were on about?" asked Billy.

"Best teacher! That's Mr. Horn," George was proud.

As Mr. Horn turned he gave George a smile and held-up his hand.

"What makes him so great?" enquired Billy.

"He's clever, he knows loads and he's a bag of fun! He also tells us great stories that he has made-up himself," continued George.

The red one went further, "He tells us all about these ghosts that haunt the classroom and leave it in a state when we're not there. He also tells us in great detail how these ghosts came to haunt him. They're friendly ghosts, most of the time but can you really have a friendship with ghosts? Oh well, it is just a story!"

Billy always wanted to know as much as he could find out from anything to do with his new environment of Skaggyness and certainly anything about a teacher he would be seeing a lot of at his new school.

Billy enquired as to who the teacher lived with while George informed him that he had never seen anyone ever go into Mr. Horn's house. In fact, George had never seen him with anyone ever at any time outside of school. Mr. Horn had told stories to the children about the ghosts of Skaggyness and in his stories the ghosts regularly followed him home and spent time in his house. As the two boys moved slowly back to number eleven and the cycles slowly passed number three, Mr. Horn closed his door behind him.

My name is Mr. Horn and the stories I tell the children in my classes about the ghosts are not stories at all, they are merely recounts of my experiences.

First, I was afraid, I was petrified, kept thinking I could never live with these ghosts by my side but then I spent so many nights thinking how they did me wrong. Then, I grew strong and I learned to get along.

Somewhat flustered and totally freaked by meeting actual real live ghosts, friendly or otherwise I have had to adjust as they have proved impossible to shake-off. However, the more time I spend with these ghosts the more I learn and sometimes they are fun as well as occasionally being extremely frightening and dangerous. I am not an expert on ghosts so I have no idea if I am doing the right thing but for some reason they picked on me, now I am clearly stuck with them.

So how did I get to be so attached with these ghosts?

As I live alone, I don't really have to worry too much about other people. I often fall asleep with the television on. I have satellite television mainly for the sport and the movies but I also watch all manner of programmes. I particularly enjoy history and one evening I was watching a whole lot of programmes on channel 666 dedicated to the Vikings. I found one programme absolutely riveting, it was all about Viking landings on Skaggyness beach and about the way a kind of Viking warrior called a berserker rampages into his opponents during battle. A berserker, from which English gets the word berserk from, would lunge into an ensuing battle to decapitate (cut-off heads) of everything in his sight during battle. Unfortunately, after viewing several back to back episodes I fell asleep outstretched on my sofa, this was quite normal for me.

The TV flickered through the night, with the sound level on the television low enough not to disturb Mrs. Diamond next door and so I could sleep through until morning if needs be. I was awoken from my slumber to the volume being slowly increased and as I peered over my snug, thick Union flag covered quilt I saw that the programme I had started watching earlier in the evening was now on the screen for a second time.

The remote control of the television had moved and was now on the floor. I hadn't left it there. Did I fall asleep with it in my hand? I thought that I had left the clicker for the screen on the desk next to my sofa...perhaps not.

I slowly rolled myself from out of the bed and picked-up the remote and placed it back on my desk, turning the TV off in order to resume my sleep. As my head hit the sweaty black cushion the television pinged back on.

The blare of the television was just audible enough for me to hear and it was definitely the same programme about Vikings landing on Skaggyness beach as had previously featured. I looked-up once more with just one-eye open searching for the control. I decided to turn the screen off on the set itself; I assumed there was some technical fault that would keep for the next day. I definitely switched the set off at the mains switch, I may have been half-asleep but I remember stumbling as I fumbled for the plug. Now I was sure I would sleep.

It was two o'clock in the morning and I had school next day. Year five could often be demanding of both energy and patience so I needed my sleep!

A minute or so passed and then…once again…the television switched itself back on!

I thought I must be dreaming, I definitely pulled the plug to the set out and then I could clearly hear the narrator describing the Vikings arriving at Skaggyness. I glanced at the mains socket and I had pulled out both plugs for the television and for the satellite box. How could this possibly be? I felt a chill come all over my body, shocking my body awake. I was compelled to listen closely to the Scottish accented voice narrating the documentary, what was so special about this programme? What was the power driving this programme on my screen?

'Around the year 800 AD King Ludd reached the east coast of England and made his way into the mouth of the Humber River. Leaving the Humber he turned into the River Trent and headed up west, probably aided by the tide, until he reached a small settlement where he and his Viking raiders disembarked.

Not so far away one Viking longship had become detached from the main attacking group of marauders and were forced to land at Skaggyness. We now know this beach as a pleasure beach with a terrific roller coaster and a fun fair, as well as its' world famous donkeys.

This group of Vikings were faced with an awaiting Saxon army who had missed Ludd's entry into the Humber but had spotted the stray longship. (A re-enactment of the supposed battle was being shown on the screen as the narrator continued.) The Vikings, hopelessly outnumbered as they ran on to the soaking sand of Skaggyness beach were slaughtered, but not instantly so. Despite facing odds of twelve Saxons to one Viking, the Vikings probably fought for a full hour before capitulating to their Saxon foe. Among the Vikings were several berserker warriors who decimated the Saxon greeting party before being overcome by sheer numbers.

The Saxons did not leave any one alive and when inspecting the longship closely they are thought to have discovered two small girls who had stowed away without their elder's knowledge. The Saxons took them back into their settlement of Skaggyness and there they remained to live and work as slaves.

The narrator continued as I became increasingly awake and somewhat baffled and horrified by the television switching itself on. I was clearly not dreaming and then I saw a slightly built grey figure. A slim grey misty figure perched on the edge of my sofa.

"Oi!" I foolishly squeaked at the figure. The vision was motionless but I clearly heard a shushing noise. The apparent ghost had me frozen stiff with my eyes not quite able to comprehend what I was seeing, my tiredness still battling with the idea that I could still be dreaming and I was being shushed in my own home! The figure slowly raised its' right-hand without making eye-contact with me and pointed for a few seconds at the screen. The ghost was watching the tele and it demanded my silence!

The narrator on the programme continued to describe the events of King Ludd's progress. The figure slowly turned its' head to face me. As it did so it was clear that the apparition was a young girl, not more than twelve, who appeared to be wearing a long dress and had hair cascading down to her waist and slightly beyond. She had her hair greasy and extensive straight at the front of her fringe, so long I couldn't see her eyes as she uttered her very first word to me, "Slaves!" she repeated the word "Slaves, Slaves, Slaves!" and then she floated off the end of the sofa and promptly disappeared into the light of flickering box that stood in the corner of the room.

The narrator on the programme was now describing the likely slave life of the two Viking girls that had been taken by the Saxons from the stray longship attacked at Skaggyness beach. Wow! I had just had my first visitation from a ghost. Not just any ghost, a Viking slave girl! I was half-glad that the figure had gone but also disappointed due to the sudden realisation that the ghost might have had zero intention of doing me any harm.

I could then hear a clanking from the kitchen next door. I dashed in and switched the lights on. A second grey figure froze and immediately dropped the bowl of cereal it had just poured for itself, the spoon and bowl hit the floor splashing milk and cereal all over my kitchen. The figure was a close resemblance of the first but with slightly older features and floated towards me and hovered as she looked into my eyes. She tried to reach out to touch my arm but her figure simply passed through my tense limb.

The ghostly figure appeared fearless of me and she passed right through my body leaving me ice-cold for a few seconds and a little weak. She turned at the door way and beckoned me to follow.

She then sat in the armchair facing the goggle box and picked up the satellite remote. The spectre wound the Viking documentary back again until the point the narrator once again described the life of the two Viking girls taken for slaves into a Saxon settlement. I sat on the edge of my sofa (I lived practically in one-room with my armchair, desk, bed and all in the same place…well I am not big on cleaning!).

The phantom figure smiled at me and raised herself from the chair. She whispered, "Like!" and then floated towards the television and just like the first figure disappeared into the screen.

I was highly excited and wide awake by now. I went into the kitchen, cleared the mess, made a cup of tea and went to my warm pillow laden pit. I was now curled up awaiting their return. They didn't return that night/morning. I got up just four-hours later, exhausted and paralysed with a mix of intrigue, fear and curiosity. I went to school with my mind spinning trying to take it all in and knowing that I couldn't discuss this with anyone without being laughed at or asked to see a psychiatrist.

I got through the day and returned home, hoping for another visitation. It was a Friday so I could happily spend my night awake seeking answers.

I spent my evening researching King Ludd and any Viking activity on the east coast of England in 800 AD. I learned all about how Ludd followed the course of the river Trent toward Nottingham leaving a trail of destruction and plunder in his wake. Ludd burnt down Nottingham Castle - according to the internet but I find that hard to believe as I don't think Nottingham Castle was even built in 800 AD - and caused devastation in the neighbourhood. I also learned that the settlement of Luddington is still a small village a few miles from Scunthorpe. I would need to do better research than just on the internet, it's not always that accurate!

From Nottingham they travelled West and fought their way through the Dove and Derwent valleys. The waters of the River Dove were clearly agreeable with the invaders as after refreshing themselves they named a place Luddswell.

I found lots of fascinating stuff about the Vikings but nothing about two slave girls or a stray longship and a battle on Skaggyness beach. I would have to try harder. The evening turned to night and I prepared myself for their visit. I waited and I waited but the night turned to light and I had seen and heard nothing.

I prepared myself every night for a week, but still nothing not a trace of Viking slave girl. I must have dreamt it, I must have done-I started to convince myself- then I was given a sign.

It was a month or so since my visitation and I arrived at school one Friday morning to be greeted in the car park by a panicking Miss Messey. Now Miss Messey was my favourite teacher in the school. She was always warm and friendly with me, not like the rest of them.

She always had a smile on her face and a kind word in all circumstances. She was the one friendly face I felt I could rely on as I entered Skaggyness Junior School each morn.

On this morning she saw me arrive and came flying out of her classroom's fire exit and over towards my car. She slammed her hands down on my bonnet and spluttered to me…"I've had ghosts in my classroom!"

Now most people would have dismissed her has having a laugh, after all it was Comic Relief day. She asked me to follow her to her classroom and she showed what she had found. She was laughing her head off as she showed me the message scrawled on her whiteboard: We love your lessons! We learn much! Your slaves Freya and Freda.

Miss Messey was now in fits of laughter as she was convinced I had written the message as a practical joke for Comic Relief day. I protested that the message was nothing to do with me. I asked her, "What lessons do you think they are talking about? Who do you think Freya and Freda are?" she had no idea. I quizzed her further and pointed out that Freya and Freda were possibly Scandinavian names…maybe Viking names.

"We're doing the Vikings, have been all term! Year three love it!" she enthused.

"There you go," I said.

"That's it! Freya and Freda are slave girls taken from their elders and captured by the Saxons when they stowed away on a longship. Their elders were slaughtered and they were discovered on the ship by the victorious Saxons. Freya and Freda were used as slave girls in the settlement of Skaggyness and now live as ghosts learning about their own Viking history from you in your lessons as they watch from the walls in your class!" I seemed to have it all figured out and said it all confidently to her as she listened to my quite logical and of course

70

experienced explanation.

Miss Messey stood looking at me with her brain doing over time as it was processing my theory, she laughed out loud and exclaimed, "It's you, you know it's you and your flippin' imagination!"

She dismissed the whole thing as me just having a laugh with her for Comic Relief day but of course you and I know that it is all true! So that was what my ghosts were doing now, watching teachers classes and no doubt watching peoples televisions for more information about their Viking past, clever ghouls!

When I arrived at my class I to found a message written on my whiteboard; Like! See soon! Freya and Freda.

I knew I would see them again. I did, but I have some more research to do now so I will have to tell you more another time. As Freya often says to me; prata snart!

Match Day

George and Billy had discovered that they both loved football. Billy had been very privileged to have watched football in all the countries he had lived in and he had lived in many different towns, cities and countries. His father was a football nut and so even on holidays if his dad could find a match he would drag Billy with him.

Billy had seen England at Wembley Stadium and he had supported some interesting teams all over Europe. He used to follow Lyon and Saint Etienne in France, Servette in Switzerland, C.S.K.A. and Lokomotiv in Russia and in Spain he was dragged to watch Real Madrid by his dad and dragged his dad to his favourite Atletico. Billy loved going to football matches, the bigger the game the better…he could never get enough!

He didn't have an English team to say he supported, he had never been in England long enough. The Three Lions (England) at Wembley was the only team he had ever seen whilst in the country. He had been escorted to Wembley every time the Ranger clan were in London to see some of his grandparents or Aunts and Uncles. He had long worked out that his father had always managed to time his trips to see family with England playing at home. Coincidence? Billy thought his dad was simply cunning in his planning!

Billy had asked George one day about Skaggyness and George explained they did have a team but he never got to watch them. He did know that they had a new manager and that they played in the Championship, but that was it. Billy, never one to be phased when in pursuit of something he wanted to know asked his dad and discovered that Skaggyness had a stadium near the train station and it was called 'The Olympic Super Store Stadium', 'figures' thought on Billy on making the discovery.

He also learned that Skaggyness had just been promoted from League One to the next level, the second-tier of English football with quiet ambitions to make the Premier League. 'Not the best level, but not a bad level!' Billy pondered. His father had planned to drag his boy to a match at the first opportunity and that day was today! The first game of the new season.

George was interested that morning to meet with Billy as they were having a little kick-about outside number eleven. Billy was full of it! He'd been learning as much as he could about Skaggyness Albion Football Club. He had already learned some of the names of the players.

"My dad says they should have a great season because they have got a new manager! Some good new players as well, so my Dad reckons!" enthused Billy sharing his delight at knowing he was going to the match that very afternoon. George was interested in anything to do with Skaggyness Albion.

Skaggyness Albion had been George's grandad's team and he used to listen to his Grandad talk about football for what seemed like every time he visited. His father had zero interest in football and George had long concluded that his dad had no interest in him either. His father's sporting passion was rugby and he detested football. George had once begged his mother to get a football magazine to be delivered every week to number one. The magazine was only delivered the one time but his dad picked it up as it came through the letter box. His father immediately binned the football mag and rang up the newsagents to stop the delivery. That was pretty much how his dad treated him and his sisters, it got worse in George's mind when his once delivered football weekly had been replaced by a rugby magazine.

"You can read this if you want something to read!" his dad threw the 'Rugby Times' magazine at him every time it came.

"Better than that rubbish you wanted!" his dad had declared.

George missed his Grandad. He hadn't heard much about football since his Grandad had died. His Grandad used to fill his head with so much information he couldn't remember all of it. Billy was now going on to George about the new manager of the Albion.

"Brian Clue is the best manager in the country my Dad reckons!" Billy relayed the boast to George.

"Brian Clue?! My Grandad used to talk about him a lot," he said somewhat enviously, truly wishing he was also going to the game.

Billy gave George his first opportunity to speak that morning." Did your Grandad ever take you to see Skaggyness Albion?"

"No, he wasn't allowed. He didn't get on with my Dad. He always said my Dad was not good enough for his daughter, my mum. My dad's a rugby fan, hates football!" George surprised Billy with that revelation. For a short breath Billy was quiet and he thrust out the

74

football for George to take. Billy then dashed indoors saying he would be back in a minute.

George was left to kick the ball against the kerb. For a moment he looked up at number ten Wibble Street. At the window he could see a boy from his school who lived there. Number ten was the home of the Dulkar family. They often went to visit family in India during school holidays so George didn't really get to know him outside of school. George gestured to the boy to come out to play football.

The boy came to the door and George went over to him. The boy was only wearing his pyjamas and socks and he beamed at George as he appeared to genuinely be pleased to see him.

"I cannot come out now we're going shopping and I am watching the cricket," said the boy.

"You can go shopping any time Sachin!" George declared.

"No chance! We're all watching the cricket anyway. My brothers and mother all have to shop for school stuff later," insisted Sachin.

Sachin had eight brothers some of them were at university but he and three others still lived at number ten.

"School will be starting soon and mother wants us all ready. With brothers like mine we have to work hard," Sachin continued.

"Okay mate. Perhaps we can do something soon," George said keen to make another pal.

Sachin smiled and explained he had to go as his father was shouting because there was a wicket in the cricket. 'I like Sachin,' thought George, 'he is pretty smart.'

Billy arrived back onto the street and raced to inform him of his news.

"My mum's rung your mum and my dad says you can go to the match this afternoon with us!" Billy proclaimed.

Tentatively George responded, "Seriously?"

"No probs, its sorted mate!" Billy affirmed.

"My Dad has become a pal of the bloke at number nine, the footballer you said that lives there," continued Billy.

"The Skaggyness player who plays for the Skaggyness Albion reserves, Cooper Robertson. He has given him some freebies, free tickets, dad was going to take Emma, my sister, but she's not bothered, so you can come instead," Billy confirmed once more.

As the penny dropped with George that he was actually going to see a football match, a Skaggyness Albion football match, a grin began to break out on his face. George and Billy had never met Cooper Robertson, although he did live in Wibble Street. Cooper Robertson had never played for the first team and with a new manager he might well never get to play for them.

The new Skaggyness Albion manager, Brian Clue, had mentioned some of the squad players in an interview to the local media. He had singled out Cooper Robertson as a player that might be on his way out of the club. Billy whipped out his smart phone and quickly found a copy of the interview on the net to share with Harry.

The report explained that Mr. Clue was surprised that Cooper Robertson and Coleraine Martin were on the transfer list – ready to move to another club. Mr Clue had watched Cooper in training and made an assessment on him. The report quoted Mr.Clue as saying;

"After watching Cooper Robertson a few times in what Cooper regarded as 'action', I am not surprised he is up for sale. Rarely has there been a more unlikely looking professional athlete. Some coaches would have taken one look, laughed – or cried – and thrown him out. He is a scruffy, unfit, uninterested waste of time. I have decided to keep him on, as well as Coleraine Martin. I don't know what it is with the dumpy little man, but something tells me is worth a last chance and I think we might find a footballer of some class inside his shuffling bulk."

Mr.Clue went on to say about Cooper Robertson that he was several kilograms over weight, indisputably he was the slowest player in the division. He went further, describing his warm-up as standing on one-leg and then swapping the weight to stand on his other leg. Mr. Clue described him as fat, often unshaven, dressed like a tramp and liked fried food to the point where he ate enough for the whole squad.

Mr. Clue summed-up Cooper Robertson as a slob an absolute slob! Despite all of these words from Mr. Clue, Cooper Robertson was going to be on the substitute's bench for today's game. The reporter had asked Cooper Robertson for a response to the manager's words. Cooper Robertson responded to Mr. Clue's assessment of him by the statement:

"I thank Mr. Clue for keeping me at the club and including me in the match day squad."

Billy had decided that Cooper Robertson might actually get on the pitch and it would be hilarious to watch a little fat footballer shuffle around the pitch making a fool of himself. George was a bit disappointed with Billy's attitude after all Cooper had given them free tickets, he deserved their support. Billy agreed that they would really get behind Cooper if he got his chance. Billy paused for thought as he remembered his very first football match.

Billy's first match was in Madrid in Spain, his father was working there and his mother worked as a teacher at Billy's school. Mr. Ranger took Billy when he was just five-years old to see Atletico Madrid play Barcelona.

Billy remembered his father holding his hand tightly as they weaved their way through the crowds. The Spanish supporters were buying different bags of sweets and nuts for snacks. Cola was seemingly free flowing, as was cerveza at all the snack bars around the ground. Billy was pushed through the turnstile and had had to wait for Mr. Ranger to squeeze his bulk through to him. He remembers a long walk up the stairs to the top tier of The Vicente Calderon and then came the moment he viewed the stadium and the crowd, it was a sensational feeling.

When Billy saw the stadium and the crowd for the first time he was hit like a thunderbolt. He remembers thinking WOW! The colour, the noise and the passion of the Atleti supporters was astounding as they continued what can only be described as a party/fiesta all the way through the game. That was it! Billy was hooked on going to the football…match day what a buzz!

Billy now hoped that George would enjoy a similar sensation in his first match.

All In The Game

The kick-off was three o'clock and just before they left the house George was handed a black and yellow scarf and put on a black and yellow sweatshirt, the colours of Skaggyness Albion.

Mr. Ranger also wore a black and yellow scarf and an adult sized sweatshirt identical to Billy's. George however was adorned in his usual red tracksuit, red trainers and red t-shirt. Mr. Ranger walked the boys to the bus stop at the end of Beach Road which was adjacent to number eleven.

They caught the number 13 bus which went very near to 'The Olympic Super Store Stadium'.

The ground was in sight of the beach; a stone's throw. As they walked towards the first programme seller Billy's father joked that perhaps some of the ex-players of Skaggyness Albion now worked as donkeys on the beach.

Mr. Ranger bought himself a match day programme and they gravitated forward edging closer to the turnstile. Loads of people all bedecked in Albion regalia were milling around the ground as the minutes to the new season started to tick by.

"There's still half-an-hour before kick-off. Do you boys want a burger?" asked Mr. Ranger.

The two boys rushed forward to the burger van and relayed to the woman serving that they wanted hot-dogs with onions. Mr. Ranger preferred the burger option. Billy noted that the burger mustard was the same colour as Albion's shirts and poured as much on as he could. He then showed George the hot dog and gave it a voice, 'Albion, Albion' he made the sausage shout.

"Can we go in now?" enquired Billy. George was taking it all in, quietly soaking up the atmosphere.

"One moment lads!" Mr. Ranger halted their progress. He patted his pockets front and back upon his person and said, "I wish I'd brought the television with us."

"Why?" asked his son.

Somewhat flustered, "Because that is where I left the tickets!"

The two boys were momentarily devastated, until a broad grin grew across Mr. Ranger's face. He brought from his wallet three tickets and waved them in the direction of the two eager beavers in front of him.

Mr. Ranger went over to the souvenir stall and had a good look at the goodies on display and the boys watched him hand over a five-pound note. The souvenir seller then handed him a scarf. He returned to the spot on which the two boys had waited and he gifted the scarf to George.

"Thanks!" the red lad responded.

"Proper fan now!" Mr. Ranger asserted.

George thought about just how great Billy and Mr. Ranger were and how lucky he was to be with them. Now he just hoped to see a great game, although it had crossed his mind that he might be best to hide his scarf when he returned home. He was worried that his father would find it and rubbish it. George wasn't sure his father would know he had been to the football as he often worked on weekends. He was guessing that only his mother knew and had given her permission for him to attend; his father never would have let him go to anything that HE didn't think was a good thing.

Mr. Ranger led them through the turnstile and watched the boys get their tickets scanned. They worked their way to their seats which were great seats exactly in line with half-way line. George was taking in the scene.

"How many people do you think are in here?" George asked.

"A few thousand!" Billy reckoned.

"The ground holds thirty-thousand and this is about half-full," Mr. Ranger estimated.

George had taken in all of Billy's pre-match build-up on board but was thinking that the crowd was quiet compared to Billy's avid descriptions of what a game is like. The fans were munching on food, reading programmes and chatting amongst themselves about what kind of game they will see today and they all seemed quite hopeful about the new season now that Brian Clue was their leader.

The public address system bellowed out the names of the team and confirmed, that their neighbour, Cooper Robertson was among the substitutes.

Mr. Ranger was giving the boys a run down on the strengths and weaknesses of each Albion player. The boys weren't really listening but George felt compelled to look as though he was listening intensely. Suddenly, Mr. Ranger launched into a joke, "Some flies were playing football in a saucer, using a sugar lump as a ball. One of them said, "We'll have to do better than this lads. We're playing in the Cup tomorrow!"

Billy groaned a disapproving groan but George beamed loving every opportunity to wear a smile.

Now the crowd were positively trembling with excitement, as Brian Clue walked out strutting like a peacock, head held high and looking as if he meant business. He wore a bottle green sweatshirt, yellow polo shirt poking up round his neck and black jog pants with striking white trainers. The crowd started to chant his name and as he stopped to put two-hands above his head to applaud the crowd a massive roar went up. George reacted to the crowd by now have a clear understanding what Billy loved so much about match day, the crowd, the event, the shared will for their team to win.

The game kicked-off and Skaggyness Albion were playing okay, gently passing the ball about in midfield and sending their wide midfielders thrusting towards the opponents goal. The opposition were quite happy to sit back and soak–up the pressure hardly bothering to break out their own half. The away team were Swadlincote Town, strugglers in the division for the past ten seasons and not really expected to win.

"Look at that!" said Billy pointing as a brave massive magpie landed on the refs shoulder. The startled ref dropped his whistle and the magpie swooped down to snatch it and flew off in the boy's direction.

"He's coming for us!" exclaimed Billy.

'Me more like!' thought George.

The magpie flew directly above George's head scraping his wing by his head before swiftly exiting the stadium complete with one shiny stolen silver referee's whistle.

"That was amazing!" noted Mr. Ranger. Billy started to wonder about the magpie. A magpie that seems to just turn-up wherever we are.

It was almost half-time and not a great deal had happened in the game. The Albion goalkeeper, Shilton Peters, had just made his first save of the match.

"England, England's number one, England's number one!" the crowd shouted in tribute to their keeper.

From the resulting corner Swadlincote, the opposition, took the lead, a glancing header at the far-post. The crowd turned angry, Skaggyness had had all the play only to see Swad score from their only attack. The half-time 'replacement' whistle went and the crowd were frustrated.

Mr. Ranger tried to cheer the boys up who were a little disappointed at being a goal down. The Ranger men and George mused over whether Cooper Robertson would get on the pitch. They all agreed Mr. Clue had to change something.

The second-half started exactly as the first one ended with Town launching an attack. Swad, clearly confident now they had taken the lead, flooded forward in numbers in a way they dare not had done in first phase of the game. Their second goal came within five minutes of the restart. Another corner, another header on the far post.

The Town fans were in raptures and started to sing their range of triumphant songs. George noted one of the chants, 'Can we play you? Can we play you? Can we play you every week?'

Mr. Clue was out of his dug-out giving instructions to his team, his substitutes were all warming-up. It was a matter of a few minutes before Mr. Clue made three substitutes which included sending on Cooper Robertson to play down the left-hand side.

George couldn't help but give Cooper Robertson the once over, "He is not as fat as I thought he was going to be!"

"But can he play George? Can he play?" demanded Billy.

The Rangers and guest gave Cooper a warm reception, applauding with great enthusiasm.

The game continued and Skaggyness started to push Swadlincote back again. The Town were happy to defend as they were two-up. There seemed to be no way through for Albion. They had Swad pegged back almost on their own goal line.

With just minutes to go the ball was sent out to the left-hand touchline by a super pass from Coleraine Martin. Robertson received the pass and immediately jinked inside the defender giving a metre of space in which to whip a perfect pass to the feet of Trevor Woodcock who shot from just outside the penalty area and everybody watched as the ball nestled beautifully in the back of the net.

Now the crowd was noisy roaring Skaggyness on, sensing a comeback. Albion continued to pour forward peppering the Swadlincote goal with shot after shot from all angles. Once again the ball came out to Robertson on the left, he flicked the ball passed the on rushing defender, and motored forward skilfully but not ever so fast. He certainly carried weight did Cooper Robertson but gosh it was clear he was the boss when the ball was at his feet. As he edged his way to goal the defenders were backing off as he was clearly a danger.

Cooper was around twenty metres from goal before playing a quick one-two with Barry Mills and with his right-foot shot to the far-post beating the outstretched goalkeeper and pinging over the line by striking the inside of the post. The crowd were ecstatic, what a comeback! Cooper Robertson what a player!

The drama wasn't over though. Sensing the win was close Albion poured forward and in the last few seconds Tony Francis was pushed over in the box and Albion were given a penalty.

The crowd slowly fell silent as they watched the Swadlincote players protest that Francis had dived and the Albion players weren't sure who was going to take the resulting penalty. Brian Clue shouted an instruction for Cooper Robertson to take the penalty. He did and without hesitation struck the ball beautifully with his left-foot to the left of the keeper who stood motionless unable to get close to Robertson's perfect pass into the goal.

The crowd were thrilled, what a game, what a manager and what a new star player Skaggyness Albion had. At the end of the game, with a 3-2 win on the first day of the season the crowd chanted the name of Mr. Clue and Cooper Robertson.

Now it was the Albion supporters chance to sing songs of triumph, "We are Skaggyness, say we are Skaggyness!"

"We're in for a great season!" declared Mr. Ranger.

"Do you want to come again?" asked Billy to George.

"Can I?" he responded with great hope in his voice, he had indeed loved his very first football match.

After the match they went back to number eleven and watched the reports on the games around the country on the television. They relived the Skaggyness match by watching the goals. They also listened to the interview with Mr. Clue who had this to stay about Cooper Robertson's performance:

"I called Robbo 'the fat man' and all sorts of bad names. As you could clearly see from his performance today if you put a ball at his feet he turns into an artist and today he painted for Skaggyness Albion a masterpiece, he is a Picasso of our game."

Billy and George now had a new footballing hero and he lived in their street!

It was time for George to go home and he asked Mrs. Ranger if he could leave his scarf there, at number eleven, and he would wear it next time he went with them to the football. A strange request she thought but she was happy to keep it safe for him.

As George was leaving, Billy was keen to set up another adventure with his mate.

"I'll call for you on Monday," Billy promised him, still clearly on a high from the excitement of the match.

"You can show me the beach!"

"Cool! See ya," George responded as he slowly walked home, sad to leave number eleven and draw closure on a great, great day. As he reluctantly strolled home he cautiously looked around and up for an escaped magpie.

The Beach

Monday morning came and Billy was delighted to see that the sun was out once again. His mum had said it was going to be a scorcher so he had stay sun safe. So Billy quickly did some personal checks:

Have I got my sun hat?

Yep, one blue sun hat.

Have I got my sun block applied?

Yep on my arms, legs, below my blue shorts and all over my face.

Now, I must remember to spend plenty of time in the shade.

Billy only needed his sunglasses and he quickly found them by his TV and his computer that sat on his large desk opposite his bed. He put on his shades and sought out a mirror to view himself. He first looked at himself in the full-length mirror that was attached to the bedroom door.

He posed a little admiring himself in his shorts, t-shirt, shades and blue baseball-cap.

"Yep, looking good!" he said to himself.

He went down the stairs towards the front door that lay at the bottom of the stairs. There was a mirror half-way down. He stopped and once again admired himself. He took off his cap and brushed his hair back several times before returning the cap to his head.

"Yep, looking very good!" he reminded himself.

As he walked towards the kitchen to look for someone to say goodbye his caught the mirror in the hall way. He couldn't resist another look. He turned to the right to check himself out, he turned to the left to pose a little more and then put his face straight on to the looking glass.

His mother, and his younger sister Emma, stood watching him stealthily from the kitchen door. He was unaware they were watching and so said to himself:

"I'm so cool I was born in a fridge! Oh yeh," he cooed.

His little sister burst out laughing and his mum smiled at him.

"You're beautiful darling! Now give me a kiss!" his mum demanded.

He pushed her away and insisted, "My kisses are for all the babes that are going to be all over me when I hit the beach!"

Emma was still giggling and was in tears as he was doing a great impression of a body builder flexing his 'non-existent' muscles and sticking his head-up in the air in a superior fashion.

"Babes! What babes! You'll be lucky if you if the donkeys look at you!" Emma teased.

Billy couldn't be bothered to retaliate so he just smirked at her and stuck his tongue out towards her. His sis replied by making a big L shape with her hand and put it to her forehead.

He pecked his mum on the cheek just as Harry was pressing the doorbell.

'I'm	walking	on	sunshine	(Wow!)
I'm	walking	on	sunshine	(Wow!)
I'm	walking	on	sunshine	(Wow!)

And don't it feel good'

The song chirped away as the doorbell was pressed.

Billy flew out the door with a quick 'see you later' for sister and mum.

"Are you Sun ready?" Billy enquired of his bright red friend.

"What do you mean?" came the response from the blue.

Billy looked his pal up and down. It was quite clear that George was either not expecting a boiling hot day or just had no idea how to prepare for it. George was wearing his customary summer's day attire; red trainers, red socks, red shorts, red t-shirt – nothing unusual there- but no hat, no sunglasses, no visible sun cream and no long sleeves to cover-up later.

"Won't your feet get hot in socks?" Billy asked.

"No! My feet get smelly if I don't wear 'em!"

Billy thought he was well trendy with no socks and sunglasses.

"Well Strawberry Skull, what we for doing?"

They quickly debated whether to walk or catch a bus to the beach.

"I've only got a pound for the phone!" insisted George in support of his argument for walking.

They agreed to walk there and Billy would shout him his bus fare on the way home.

They headed down Beach Road, a long two-mile straight stretch all the way to Skaggyness Beach. They rested on benches along the way as both boys were flagging in the ever increasing heat of the morning.

As they got within easy sight of the sea they took a rest where Billy insisted on buying a couple of ice-pops.

"Only a week before school starts again," George commented.

Billy was aware of starting his new school and there was a good chance he would find himself in the same class as new friend.

"What's it like? Skaggyness Junior School," enquired Billy.

"It's alright…for a school," George lethargically replied.

"Watch out for certain teachers though; they can be quite difficult and a bit boring!"

George told Billy all about certain teachers, Mrs. Whatfor and the Headteacher…Mr Smythe. George was clearly not impressed by much about his school.

"What about the other children?" Billy continued his enquiry.

"Yep, they're fine," George asserted.

Actually, George didn't really know many of the children that well; he wanted to know them but found it difficult to make friends. George was not unpopular at school though, lots of children thought he was a pleasant boy but awfully quiet. It had started to cross George's mind, that when they started school in Year 6 the following week, he would have to share his one friend; 'I think he's going to be popular' thought George.

Billy had thought about his new pal a lot, when he wasn't being haunted by the thought of Mickey Magpie in whatever form he had taken. He had decided that he wanted to be a good friend to George but he had hoped that not all the children were like him.

Billy was looking forward to hitting the beach but the visit was part of his plan to try and take George out of the boundary wall that surrounded Skaggyness. The wall itself extended only so far into the sea and so Billy figured it would be easy to drift their vessel beyond the wall, so his mission would be accomplished.

Billy planned to have all the fun the beach had to offer, with his pal but he was clear that if they could hire a boat he would steer it with George passed the jutting wall. Billy was working towards this with the full-knowledge he would have to pay for the boat and sneakily get George to go along with his plan. Billy couldn't be sure of the reasons that George had shown so much resistance to the idea of leaving the town boundary, even for a moment. Billy wasn't convinced it could all be fear of his father; fear of the unknown maybe? Billy was determined to get his new pal over this little problem, he didn't want a big chicken as his pal arriving at his new school.

As the two finished the long walk they first played football with some much younger boys and girls for a few minutes. It was a very light beach ball and nobody seemed to have much control over it.

When the younger kids were called over by their mum, Billy and George looked for the next activity. They spotted the donkey rides and made their way towards them.

'Two pounds for fifteen minutes' the sign read.

Billy offered to pay for George, with Billy thinking about how much more fun Skaggyness would be if he could find pals who also had pocket money to have fun with.

"No need," said George.

To Billy's amazement George approached the man with the donkeys. The man wore a grey cowboy hat and had half a cigarette hanging out from his mouth. He was scruffy and clearly hadn't had a shave for a couple of days. The man wore a red neck-chief and had a handlebar moustache. His dress was completed with frayed jeans and flip-flops. Billy concluded that the man didn't make fortunes from donkey rides as to him he didn't look as though he had had a good meal in days as he was so thin.

George's conversation with the man was a cunning one and Billy was mightily impressed with the outcome.

George offered to follow the donkeys for the next half-an-hour and scoop up any donkey poo for the man in exchange for a ride; the man agreed.

For the next half-an-hour George followed the donkeys; trailing them armed with a short handled shovel and a big bucket.

He got in as close he could and followed with his huge poop scoop and crouched down as he awaited the donkeys' offerings hoping he might catch it before they hit the floor.

When it did come George wasn't quite quick enough to catch it and spent a good portion of his time scraping it from the sand with a little bit of splash back on his red...now reddy brown trainers. He collected it all in a sack and dragged it back to the starting point of the donkey ride. The half-hour elapsed and, though he had an aching back, Harry made it on to the donkey of his choice. He was duly joined by Billy together they enjoyed their jaunt. They pretended they were a pair of cowboys shooting at the seagulls up above them.

"That's weird," noted Billy.

"One of the seagulls looks a lot like a magpie," but they were too high-up in the air for them to get a clear view. George did not need much convincing.

George smiled wildly as the donkey took each step. Billy soon got bored as George went quiet after the discovery of a circling magpie. George was perched tall in the stirrups as if he was the proudest boy on the beach.

"I didn't even have to pay!" George reminded his pal. 'Errrm', thought Billy, 'but you paid in sweat!'

The fifteen-minutes elapsed and they both dismounted before waving to the donkey man.

"Cheers!" shouted George.

Billy commented that it was time for them to head towards the other side of the beach where there were boats for hire. Billy was ready to hatch his next plan on how to get George to the outside of Skaggyness. He had already tried getting him to cycle out of an exit but failed miserably. What about floating beyond the boundary while out at sea? Billy was plotting his course of action with George completely unaware of the agenda.

They eventually came to some boats and Billy convinced George that they should hire a boat.

Armed with a plan, Billy addressed the dreadlocked gentleman tethering a rowing boat to the side of the wall stretching into the sea, "I'd like to hire one of your motor boats please."

"Can you afford it?" the man enquired.

"I just want it for half-an-hour," Billy assured the man.

"It would be £10 for half-an-hour but I can't let you have one!"

"Why not?"

"You and you're buddy are too young man, I can only let the motor boats out to adults," the man informed him. 'Blast! Spanner in the plan!' thought Billy.

Billy still had over fifteen pounds in his pocket and asked about the rowing boats, he drew a blank once more when the man said he wasn't strong enough to handle the rowing boats and he only let them go to sixteen-year-olds and above. Billy's plan wasn't going as well as he thought it would.

Billy pulled an agonising face and read the man's name badge – Eddie – it read, it prompted a fresh approach to the man from Billy.

Billy was worried he wasn't looking such a big man in front of his highly impressionable young pal.

Billy launched into a meaningful patter with Eddie, "Now, Eddie, we're both men of the world, you have boats, I have money, capish?"

"What can you have me and my fire bunny friend have for a fee?"

"You can have a pedalo little man," the man gestured towards a large plastic yellow rubber duck with pedals.

Billy had been on a pedalo before and knew they were hard work and quite slow but what else could he do?

The man took ten-pounds for half-an-hour and insisted both Billy and George wore a fluorescent orange life-jacket.

Billy was busy explaining to George how the pedalo worked; "You have to power the boat by pedaling as hard as you can and that in turn pushes a paddle-wheel under the boat,"

George took his position side-by-side with his fellow ship mate. They pedaled and pedaled and pedaled without making much progress. 'We've only got this for thirty minutes and we don't appear to be moving very much,' thought Billy.

They slowly edged towards the edge of the wall where Billy was planning to breach the Skaggyness boundary. They kept going straight alongside the inside of the wall, the boat was banging into the wall periodically. George started to argue with Billy.

"Why don't we go over there towards that little island near where all the other boats are? It's not much fun against the wall!" suggested George, this would be well away from the wall and well within the town boundary.

Billy insisted that they stay near the wall, it was the only way he could guarantee breaching the boundary in the time they had. As the edge of the wall came into view Harry started to protest.

"We've had over fifteen minutes now, we better turn back."

"No we're alright…we'll turn in a minute," insisted Billy.

"No we've got to go back, I can't pedal anymore," George responded.

The pedalo bobbed forward as George refused to pedal insisting on heat exhaustion.

The pedalo reached the edge of the wall and Billy suddenly burst into a furious pedal to take him passed the boundary and out of the Skaggyness zone.

"Come on! Pedal!" Billy suddenly ranted.

George was motionless as he watched his pal pedal furiously but achieving only in spinning the pedalo in a circular movement. With only one person pedaling the pedalo simply went around and around in a circle.

Billy was getting angry, "Why won't you go for it? Why won't you pedal passed the boundary wall. We could do it now! You can get out of the Skaggyness zone!"

"Don't want to, not allowed. My Dad will know, I need to go back."

With this George stood-up and dived into the sea and swam back to the beach in the Skaggyness zone.

Billy was stunned. He couldn't believe it! Not only had he failed yet again to persuade George to leave the town's walled area, his new pal had just left him out at sea alone with a pedalo! A magpie perched itself on the back of the pedalo and in a flash George stood up and dive bombed in the water. As if possessed, he swam an awkward swim hampered by fear, life jacket, clothes and shoes he reached the beach it what could have been world record time. Billy opened mouthed stared in wonderment!

Billy had no choice but to strip to his undies and dive in the water himself grab the attached rope at the front and pull the pedalo back to the beach. It was a struggle and he didn't seem to be getting very far.

George had reached the beach, it was obvious he was a strong swimmer. Billy had noticed and was very impressed with his speed and strength. George was seen telling the boat man that Billy was out on his own with the pedalo. The boat man was quickly out to him in one of the unrented motor boats with George aboard heading towards Billy. The magpie hitched a lift for a while but flew off as soon as Eddie and the motor boat got close.

It didn't take more than two-minutes before the boat man pulled alongside Billy into the boat. He quickly tied the pedalo to the side of the boat and in no time at all they were all safely back on the beach.

Billy was quite bemused by the events that had just unfolded. He felt for sure he could get George outside of the wall surrounding Skaggyness for the first time in his life and that he would thank him for it. Billy couldn't understand his reluctance; why wouldn't he go beyond the Skaggyness zone? Billy was even more perplexed and suspicious about their magpie stalker!

Eddie gave them both a lecture about safety in the water and gave them towels. He directed them to his small hut where they could get a bit drier and in Billy's case dressed.

Billy gathered up his clothes from the pedal and took up Eddie on his offer. George passed up the chance and said that the Sun was so hot he'd be dry in minutes.

The two didn't speak to each other as their friendship was now slightly uneasy.

The Short Long Way Home

The two boys walked away from the boats and made their way up the beach. They stayed close to each other but both were enduring the longest silence they had ever known between them.

They lumbered up the beach, both began to wilt under the burning sun. They reached the road and Billy stopped at the bus stop to read the timetable to work out when he could get a bus back to Wibble Street. George walked passed the bus stop and appeared to be on automatic pilot as his head never lifted, guided by his soul, ambling back down the way he came towards home.

"Oi!" Billy broke the silence.

"You're on the bus with me!" Billy reminded George of his promise.

"Didn't think you would do it for me," George mumbled.

"You're still a mate! So come and help me work out when the buses are."

"They're every half-hour from seven o'clock in the morning until eleven at night," George informed him.

"It's the V1 you need."

"Great!" Billy quickly checked his watch (it was all misted up from his swim), as George glanced at his only to remember that he didn't actually own a watch.

Billy noted the time and worked out that there was just six minutes before the four o'clock bus was due. He took a good look at George, he didn't look well. The sun had clearly been busy while the two boys were at play and Billy was convinced that his pals 'tomato head' would explode.

"Are you okay? Do you feel alright?" enquired Billy, somewhat concerned.

"To be honest, I feel really ill! My head hurts and I am burning!" George complained.

"You've probably got sun stroke!" Billy suggested.

Billy noted how he hadn't stayed sun safe.

Billy gently grabbed his arm and moved him to the shade of the bus stop.

"Wait there!" Billy instructed.

Billy dashed across the road to the shop and within a third minute had returned with two bottles of ice-cool water. Billy gestured to George to take one of the bottles. Billy was also quite hot and didn't hesitate to poor half the bottle on his head before guzzling the rest. George responded by copying Billy's movements.

"You look like a stick of rhubarb!" Billy commented, although he kind of always looked a little bit like a stick of rhubarb he thought.

Certainly amused, "Got any custard?" remarked George.

As they started to laugh the bus pulled-up. Billy did the honours with the money and they both made their way down to the back of the bus.

The back of the bus was already taken by a group of teenage girls. George spotted them and realised who they were. George tugged on Billy's blue shirt as he worked his way towards the girls. George pulled it so hard Billy had no choice but to look around and George pulled on him even harder to sit on the nearest seat half–way down the half-empty single-decker.

As they both thudded down on the seat, George whispered, "Don't go near those girls that are sitting at the back!"

Somewhat disappointingly, "Why?"

"That's some of the 'House of the Seven Sister's' " George informed him of the reasoning of his actions.

Billy was savvy enough not to look round at the girls, but was becoming ever more curious as to what was so scary about these girls from number seven (and six) Wibble Street. George didn't look round, rigid from fear not because he was streetwise.

The girls were talking amongst themselves, seemingly quite harmlessly.

Billy was straining his ears desperate for clues as to work out the cause of their seeming infamy but all he could hear was two old ladies discussing the merits of the brand new Olympic hypermarket.

'What do I care that they sell the cheapest baked beans in the town' Billy thought.

There was no conversation between the two boys as George was stiff with fear, and probably sunstroke, while Billy was acting the Sherlock. As the bus approached the top of Wibble Street, George grabbed Billy's arm and gestured for him to get off the bus. Billy didn't question why they were getting off at the stop before the top of Wibble Street.

The two boys got off and watched the bus and the girls go by.

"I take it we have got off early to avoid the girls!"

"Got it in one!" replied George.

As the bus started to disappear passed them, the back window appeared to be full of hand gestures…or was it waving? The boys noted that a magpie, or even the magpie had perched itself on the top of the bus; it appeared to be using its' wings to make the same gesture to the boys.

They only had a short walk back to Wibble Street and George was going to be glad to get home.

"Do you think you'll be okay to come out tomorrow?"

"I hope so!" George noted.

"We haven't got many days left before school now," Billy reminded him.

"No, just a few days," George concurred.

"I take it you have something you want to do," George surmised.

"Yeh," Billy smiled, realising how quickly George had got to know him.

"I want to go back into Wobbling Wood, there is more adventure in that place I am sure," Billy said confidently.

"It's dangerous," George said.

"It's magical!"

"No, it's dangerous!" repeated George.

They agreed to review it all the next day to consider their health and well- being but Billy had already made their mind-up for them.

First thing in the new morning Billy was on the phone calling for George to get his red trainers on and thrill seek. However, a quick conversation with George's mum put the mockers on Billy's plans as she informed him George was still unwell.

"Does he like custard?" Billy asked Mrs. Forest.

"Yes he does, why?" she asked.

"Oh no reason, just tell him I asked," Billy switched his phone off grinning away to himself as he pictured George as a stick of rhubarb and his mum pouring cold custard all over him.

Billy would put his plans on hold, at least for a day.

Squibbits

The two boys picked-up their adventures the very next day as the new school term was stealthily closing in. Now looking a little less flushed, George had recovered sufficiently to partner Billy in another trek into the mysterious Wobbling Wood. Billy meanwhile was carrying a fairly large black rucksack – he had come equipped for adventure.

"What's in the bag?" George enquired.

Billy was a little cautious with his answer, "Picnic and stuff."

On their previous visit to the wood, George did not get to meet a squibbit, a creature of human stature but made-up of half-squirrel and half-rabbit. Billy was hoping that they would make an appearance once again because he had questions to ask about the wood. They entered the wood and followed the track.

As the wood deepened and the boys had fun bouncing off the trees, looking out for the secrets of the life of the wood in the surroundings. They were heading back towards the golden shed, a seemingly well-trod path by heavy animals judging by the paw and hoof prints they were tracking through the wood.

They came upon a clearing and Billy suggested they sat down for a rest and pause to observe the life of the splendid tree collection. George agreed and they sat on a fallen tree stripped of its' branches.

Billy insisted on hush as they both keen-eyed scanned and skimmed their eyeballs across the sky, the trees and the bushes. They were listening for any kind of rustling or movement. A large magpie flew down and landed just a metre from their feet.

Without warning the now familiar furry paw was placed on Billy's shoulder and although both boys sprang off the log and onto to their tip-toes George ran while Billy turned to smile and greet the squibbit.

George Belted into the trees and you could hear the thudding of his feet and the rustling of the plants as he bolted away from the creature.

Decidedly unimpressed, "Don't worry about him Razor, he'll come back in a minute when he sees everything is okay," Billy assured his friendly squibbit.

"I wondered if you two boys would ever return," continued Razor.

"I was never going to let you get away without sharing some secrets with me," said Billy.

"Secrets? What secrets?" asked Razor, the chief of all squibbits in Wobbling Wood.

"Come on! You must know that there are no animals like you anywhere in the world, except here! You must share the stories of how you came into existence," insisted Billy.

Razor was quite at ease with Billy as the boy offered to share his picnic from his bag. Billy presented Razor with a handful of nuts but Razor just smiled.

"Wow you have such small nuts!" Razor blurted out.

Billy thought about the size of the nuts the squibbits were passing around last time they met. 'Razor has got a point' Billy thought. Razor took the whole lot and popped them into his mouth.

Emerging from the trees and back into the sun drenched clearing came George - the magpie had long fluttered off.

"I have come back to see if you are okay," George said.

"Did you enjoy your exercise?" asked Razor.

"Yes…exercise…very good!" George replied.

He sat down with them as they shared round the fizzy drink.

Razor had problems with the bubbles and insisted the orange drink they had given him was not good for a squibbit.

"So you want to know about the wood and the squibbits do you?" Razor asked.

Both boys nodded in awe of Razor this man-sized, grey furred, floppy-eared with huge incisors talking creature.

"Well this wood has a long and dark history," Razor began.

"We have had many battles to survive here. Many wars and we are always on alert!" Razor continued.

Razor explained that the grey squibbits had had many wars with the red squibbits but the greys currently have the wood to themselves. He went on to explain how other creatures come to the wood from the air and from the under growth to challenge their kind.

The boys were hanging on his every word. "My own story is also quite a tale. Would you like to know how I might met my wife?" Razor asked, a story he never got tired of telling.

"If you like, yes please tell us! Details and all, it's all amazing! A whole new world for us!" Billy shrieked.

Razor started his yarn:

When my father, Floppy Simon (the second most important chief…'Floppy' being a squibbit title equal to a human Duke in England) was banished by my uncle, Floppy Fred (the number one chief) and many loyal grey squibbits followed him into Wobbling Wood. They settled here as they had drifted from Beston Forest. Here they lived simply, gathering nuts and wild fruits. The wood gave them a leafy roof, and mossy beds to kip on.

Floppy Simon found himself happier than he had ever been before.

Floppy Fred's life was not turning out to be so great. He was riddled with painful guilt, and started to grow suspicious of all those around him, especially his nephew, me!

I had not gone into exile with my father as my cousin Blade, a one born, had begged me to stay as we only had each other as trustworthy play mates. My cousin and I were firm friends.

As we grew into young adulthood, Floppy Fred noticed how I outshone Blade, his own son. I had my shiny rich grey fur and my gorgeous brown eyes. I attracted far more admirers than Blade who had scruffy light grey fur and diagonal teeth.

Floppy Fred's resentment of me ate away inside him. Fred was determined that if I gave him even a slight reason, he would banish me, just like my father.

The squibbit paused to wipe his brow with his ears and seemed to wipe a tear from his eye.

"Please go on," requested Billy, rather selfishly, not caring about the strain of telling such a story.

Razor carried on the tale…well one fine morning, Blade and I visited a hedgehog fair on our way home from nut gathering. There we met the Boo, one of Floppy Fred's loyal servants.

"Boys, you are just in time!" Boo announced. "The good Floppy

Fred has offered a prize of a bag full of acorns to any squibbit who can fight and beat his personal bodyguard Atlas the Great! Two squibbits had already been dragged away from Atlas, all battered and missing chunks of fur.

The last challenger was, strangely, a sweet looking young squibbette. Everybody wanted her to win, but it was more likely that Atlas would squash her rather too easily!

Blade and I were completely mesmerised by this brave squibbette and followed her to the small arena that Boo had constructed from oak branches.

By that time quite a crowd had gathered around the square that had been marked out on the grass. Within the square stood Atlas the Great! His incredibly powerful shoulders and broken nose made the massive squibbit seem more like a gorilla than a squibbit.

Floppy Fred showed himself from the crowd as he stepped forward towards his son and I. He shook Blade's hand and hugged him manly. I however, was not noticed.

"I'm so pleased you're here," said the floppy.

"A brave but perhaps foolish stranger of a squibbette has insisted on fighting my personal bodyguard. I cannot persuade her to change her mind, but perhaps you, my courageous son may!" my uncle thought.

Uncle Fred instructed the Boo to fetch the foolhardy squibbette; while my uncle took his place in the umpire's chair by the side of the square.

The young squibbette the Boo presented to Blade and I was dressed in a dark purple cape and black mask over her eyes. She was not slightly built herself, she was taller than both Blade and I, with most sensational cascading blonde fur ears that flopped over her shoulders in a fool-around manner.

She had two gleaming white incisors and clear blue eyes. I felt dizzy whenever I was in her line of sight.

"Do you really intend to fight the floppy's own personal bodyguard, miss?" Blade asked of her.

"I do, kind sir," said the squibbette.

"I can then only wish that you wouldn't," my cousin begged.

I too came forward and begged her not to fight 'Atlas the Great!'

I blurted out to her how she might have her beautiful face and gorgeous everything …I stopped myself from spilling more compliments before pointing out that Atlas may kill her!

The squibbette smiled. She said how touched she was by my cousin's and my concern.

"I need the bag of acorns, I need them!" she stressed.

"If I am hurt or even die, then so what? I have no family or friends to care for now whether I live or die."

I kept my thoughts to myself, but I thought how much I instinctively cared for such a beautiful creature.

One small squibbit standing close to the floppy started to blow a trumpet chorus and the two gladiators emerged into the centre of the square.

My uncle shouted, "Three, two, one…fight!"

The two squibbits circled around the square waiting for each other to make an error and create an opportunity to lunge.

Atlas started to make many grabs but each time the squibbette avoided the paws, gracefully moving from side-to-side like a ballroom dancer. Atlas appeared to be lumbering compared to his fair opponent. Some of the crowd began to titter at the square powerful shouldered squibbits' expense. Atlas was losing his temper as the laughter was beginning to grow. Atlas made more attempts to grab the squibbette but he was more and more careless as his fury grew and grew.

The stranger was now ready to make her move. Swiftly she seized Atlas around his waist. She raised him off the floor and threw him on to the ground. There Atlas lay stunned and winded.

The crowd went wild with surprise and delight, until the moment Floppy Fred stood erect from his seat and signalled for silence.

My Uncle was angry, very, very angry. He demanded to know the identity of Atlas's conqueror.

The squibbette revealed herself to be Natalia youngest daughter of Great Buck Vladimir the Red, the crowned buck of the red squibbits. My uncle's face was thunder but he could not dishonour his pledge to any victor in front of such an audience. In his fury, Uncle Fred bellowed, "Your dead father was my sworn enemy!" he spat his words as he threw a bag of acorns at the feet of the squibbette, "Now take your nuts and go!"

My Uncle grabbed my cousin by the hand and dragged him off with Boo closely following. Blade was embarrassed at his father's actions as he trailed in his wake.

The crowd dispersed to leave only Natalia and I. I stepped forward and took a lump of fur from my rear and gave it to her. This action is an esteemed token of love and respect between squibbits, not historically established between the grey and the reds of the species.

She said she would keep it always to remember the day and my kind words that I had shared with her earlier that morn.

I told her, "Fair Natalia I once knew your father, he was a proud squibbit!"

She reached slightly down towards my face and stroked my rounded cheeks.

Behind me, Boo appeared and he asked her why the regal daughter of Vladimir was wrestling at the hedgehog fair. She explained how her older sister Olga refused to let her share the nuts in their area of the forest. She had driven her to seek nuts in this manner and that she had sworn to destroy her if she ever went back.

Now her identity was known to all, Boo explained to her how she was no safer here than she was on the other side of Beston Forest.

"Floppy Fred is in one of his darkest moods and he means to do you harm if you stay here," claimed Boo.

I listened to Boo pleading with her to go to Wobbling Wood and seek my father's protection. Natalia responded and turned to ask my name. "Razor" I whispered, "Razor…Floppy Simon's son."

"Sharp," she smiled at me sweetly before claiming mine a wonderful name.

As Natalia said my name, danger was galloping towards her.

Razor and Blade

Billy and George continued to listen in amazement of this ace storytelling squibbit. They munched their way through all their food and were now guzzling their fizzy stuff.

Razor continued his story. When Natalia left for Wobbling Wood I felt I had fallen in love with her. I sought out my cousin, Blade for company. I shared my thoughts and feelings with him. Blade could not accept how I was feeling about Natalia as I had only just met her.

I was smitten for my dear Natalia. My Uncle Fred appeared, his face contorted into a raging frown.

"Leave my forest Razor!" he raged.

"You have five nights from this night to flee my forest! If I find you within ten miles of my forest I'll have you hunted down for your very grey fur and gut you for a magpie's meal!" my charming uncle promised me. George went pale with the idea of being a magpie's meal.

I quizzed my uncle what I had done to deserve this threat but he insisted that the sight of me talking to a daughter of his sworn enemy had made his stomach turn. Uncle Fred was convinced we were plotting to kill him and return my father to be chief squibbit in Beston Forest.

I pleaded with him to believe that no such plot was afoot but he would not have it. Blade joined in my protestations but there was no placating Floppy Fred. My uncle turned on me saying how I mocked his son as inferior and would do him harm as I would him as well.

The Floppy marched out on us repeating his five-night warning.

Blade and I decided that I must flee Beston Forest at once and head for Wobbling Wood to seek my father. Blade insisted on coming with me, he wished to flee his ever growing mad father and he had never known a life without me.

We decided the best way to stay safe and avoid my uncle coming after us was to wear a disguise so we wore hedgehog skins. We decided that we would travel with false names, I would be Gillette and Blade would be Wilkinson.

Some weeks later, my father was entertaining his band of merry squibbits around a camp fire. They were being careful not to scorch their precious fur, as they roasted their nuts for a rare kind of feast.

Natalia had found Floppy Simon at last. She advanced into the light of the fire as darkness shone all around the wood. She raised her hands to the strangers of the light to show she had no weapon.

"Forgive me! I had given myself up as abandoned until I saw your flames," she announced.

My father demanded an answer as to why she was there.

"I seek Floppy Simon," she declared.

"You seek no more squibbette, sit!" my father demanded.

"Who are you squibbit wench?" he continued.

Tentatively and with a large gulp of air, Natalia declared herself a daughter of the Great Buck Vladimir the Red. My father had no doubt as to her claim of identity. Floppy Simon had been well aquainted with her father.

"I see much of him in you fair squibbette!"

My father instructed her to sit and share the nuts, "tell your tell story and be quick about it, the cold draws ever closer."

Meanwhile, Blade and I were making our own way through Wobbling Wood. For over a month we had been living in a discarded badger set on the very edge of the wood. We had fed on an abundance of nuts, carrots and fruit that grew all around the edge of the wood and backed onto a farm.

I grew ever frustrated as my thoughts for Natalia were left unsatisfied and my search for my father had not been successful.

I fretted that the moment for Natalia and I had passed. Blade tried to convince me that if love was there love would stay. I had seen love in fair Natalia's eyes, love for me I was sure.

Billy was smiling with a lovely grin on his mush as he mulled over the open way of Razor's love story. George was polite and attentive but was also looking for the sick bag at the soppy nature of the tale.

Razor was still yarning...

Blade and I were strolling into the wood further than we had ever dare venture when we heard a rustling and a murmur. We hid and then bravely took a peek towards the noise. To our delight it was fair Natalia herself!

I almost screamed with joy at the sight of her. She was bending down gathering some fine looking nuts.

Blade pushed me forward and dared me to carpe diem! (Seize the day).

"Go cousin! Share your feelings!"

As the bushes parted I dropped my hedgehog skin and I was left face to face with Natalia.

We stood there staring at each other motionless and silent.

Natalia spoke first, "When I can't control my behaviour, it's because my heart belongs to Razor!"

I followed that up with an exchange of, "I want to get inside the heart and head of Natalia my beautiful red."

Natalia showed me the fur I had given her and we embraced.

For the next day we talked, walked and stalked our emotions.

I asked Natalia to marry me.

I wanted Blade to share our joy. I had hoped he would also find love on our journey but that was sure to happen to such a loyal type. "It all seems a bit rushed to me," evoked Blade.

Natalia explained she must return to dine with Floppy Simon.

"Floppy Simon is near?"

"Yes, his camp is quite close."

"Then we must leave at once to see my father once again."

With that I gripped fair Natalia's paw and we sped together to the camp without thinking we left Blade behind alone at the abandoned badger's set.

Blade, however was not alone for long. He too had discarded his hedgehog disguise. He was soon approached by a tall, strong looking red squibbette.

"Are you Blade?" the squibbette gushed.

"That I am!" responded Blade.

The red squibbette showed him a picture of Natalia.

"I seek fair Natalia, I am told you have knowledge of her."

"Perhaps, but who is she to you?" enquired Blade.

"I am Olga, sister to Natalia."

Olga explained how she had set out on the trail of her sister to make her peace with her and invite her back to Beston Forest to feast on the best nuts the forest had to offer. Blade sat and told Olga of the events of the past month or so and that her sister had found solace in his own fair cousin that was myself, Razor.

Olga had started to eye Blade in the same manner that I had always looked upon Natalia. By the time they had strolled to meet with us at the camp of Floppy Simon they too had found each other.

The evening was spent with Floppy Simon, his band of merry squibbits, myself, Natalia, Blade and Olga celebrating the yield of events in Wobbling Wood. The very next day Floppy Simon nominated a large tree as a chapel tree. Natalia and I were married by the chapel tree. After my father had given us his blessing, Olga and Blade declared their love for each other and they to insisted on a blessing of marriage by the chapel tree.

Floppy Simon was the happiest of us all as he was just elated to have me back by his side and had gained a daughter to boot. As we began a celebratory feast a galloping squibbit pulled-up to our group. It was Boo, all the way from Beston. An exhausted Boo told us of events back in Beston.

"My esteemed master, Floppy Fred this morning has come to the edge of Wobbling Wood with his grey army seeking vengeance on your band."

"He meant to slay you all and all your joy. Instead, he met a holy hedgehog who spoke to him prickly piercing words of wisdom. As a result, Floppy Fred returns your status as Chief Squibbit of Beston Forest. He has given up his Floppydom and joined a hedgehog monastery. This my Floppiness leaves you as our supreme chief and you must return to Beston Forest to govern all the grey armies."

"Tonight we celebrate and you are welcome to join us Boo," my father asserted.

"At first light we will tidy our wood and return to our friends in Beston Forest."

With that Razor stood-up. "Are you going?" asked Billy.

"Yes, we will speak again," and with that Razor hopped off into the trees.

The two boys looked at each other. "What now fair George?"

"Let's wander fair Billy!" and so they rose and then wandered.

Lost

The two boys roamed through the wood. Silently and aimlessly they wandered deep into the forestry. They said nothing as they both enjoyed the noise of wood life and soaked up the rays of the sun that intermittently hit the floor through the gaps in the trees.

Some minutes passed before George broke the silence. "Where are we going?"

"I don't know! I was following you!"

With surprise George responded, "Ooh! I was following you!"

"Where are we?" asked Billy.

"I have absolutely no idea!" George declared.

It suddenly dawned on them both that they had absolutely no idea where they were. Neither of them knew the wood well enough to find their way back with any amount of ease.

Together, they announced to each other that they were lost.

They agreed to keep walking until they saw something that might give them a notion of how to get back. They hadn't planned to sit with Razor and listen to his story; even though they both really enjoyed it. Razor's monologue had thrown Billy off from his original plan.

Without knowing it the two had meandered from their intended pathway.

Like a homing beacon the glimmering gold of Billy's sought out shed was pulling them towards it. They ambled, they weren't sure where, but it was towards a clearing and soon enough they came across the all that glitters was definitely the gilded shack.

"Here we are!" announced Billy as he clapped eyes on the gleaming hut.

"Oh no! We are not going in there again!" protested George, second guessing Billy's plans.

"Let's just have a look again, it's a curious place, worth investigating," Billy insisted.

"I got hurt last time," George reminded him.

Billy quickly reminded George, "You got cleaner and stronger as well! At least for a while before the 'power of the hole' wore off." Harry deliberated over how the incident in the hole last time had indeed given him some form of extra power, for an hour or two before the effects wore off.

"It'll be alright!" Billy insisted.

They both approached the door and Billy reached for the handle.

As Billy's hand came within a centimetre of the shiny knob and an almighty roar came from within the golden shed. The two boys were thrown back onto their bottoms and again the roar came from within the interior of the shed but the glistening outhouse was now shaking.

The two boys were stunned.

"I was not expecting that!" declared Billy.

George had scuttled into a cowering position behind Billy. "Can we go now?" asked our red hero.

As the two boys pondered their next move they watched the shed as the golden blinds that took the place of the panes suddenly disappeared creating a window without glass. Billy suddenly realised they would be able to access the hole, if they were swift.

Suddenly at the window's ledge were two wieldy looking paws appearing to flop over the side with an almighty thud. The roar had appeared not to phase Billy from his mission and the sight of these two huge muscular snowy white furry paws didn't deter him either.

George had by now developed a vice-like grip on Billy's jacket as he curled up tight desperate to see but not be seen. Billy, shaken but not stirred listened carefully as he whispered, "I've got a bad feeling about this!"

The door of the Golden Shed evaporated and the paws disappeared from the ledge. Within a couple of seconds, as the boys sat motionless, the huge cat carefully and sure footedly walked on all fours through the glittering exit. The boy's eyes were transfixed on the feline. Billy's brain was trying to comprehend both its' appearance and his next move. George clung tight, still trying even harder to make himself disappear.

Billy was convinced that it was a lioness, a huge lion, but he spied its' markings and white fur in places. The giant feline slowly circled the boys sniffing the air as it did so. George had his face screwed-up and buried into the back of Billy. Billy's eyes never left the head of the stalking cat as it wafted its' tail. After taking a good look and smell of the two petrified children, the liger walked carefully back towards the shed. The massive animal turned and approached Billy head-on, putting its' huge over whiskered bonce ever so silently towards Billy's face. Billy was terrified but daren't show it as fear had taken over his body, the huge head was now nose-to-nose with him. 'Bad breath!' ...needs a mint or mouthwash or something thought Billy trying to regain control over his relatively puny human frame.

Slowly, the creature lifted its' front paws and moved to rear-up onto its hind legs. The huge powerful looking cat now stood on two legs, arms folded looking downward upon the boys. Billy carefully started to lift his eyes from the ground where he followed the body of the animal from its feet, up past the white and black striped stomach, eventually resting his eyeballs on the under-side of the chin.

The creature began to speak, "Why are you here?"

"We wanted to explore inside the shed," murmured Billy.

"We're not that bothered though!" exclaimed George, Billy's back muffling his cries.

"I am Lancer, the guardian of the labyrinth. The Golden Shed is my guard box. You cannot just wander in when you feel."

"We have been before," Billy said his brain flashing wildly as the liger had just informed him that this HOLE was the entrance to a labyrinth; a darkened network of mysterious alleys and treasures?

"And I didn't like it!" piped-up a quivering George, at the same time he thought what's a labyrinth?

Lancer continued, "You got lucky then didn't you!"

"I guard the paths, the passages and the secrets of the labyrinth," explained Lancer.

Billy asked, "What are the secrets of the labyrinth?"

"Wouldn't you like to know?" Lancer responded.

"The secrets are many and the powers are great, when they choose to show themselves," continued the mighty looking beast.

George's face now appeared over Billy's shoulders, convinced they would not be eaten at that precise moment.

"Can you show us around? We would be ever so grateful," George quizzed and stated.

"Show you around! SHOW YOU AROUND! I am the EVIL GUARDIAN not the tour guide!"

"If I catch you down there I will have to …well…do what I am paid for! And when I am awake I am always hungry!" Lancer said menacingly, then he let out a huge roar.

The boys were calculating their next move, George looking for retreat and Billy still looking to advance into the labyrinth.

"Are you a lion?" queried Billy, hoping to keep the animal friendly.

"A lion, a lion? Look at my stripes!" Lancer threw his front legs wide open in arm fashion and twirled for the boys to see his hard-to-see black stripe pattern all over his white fur.

"You're a white tiger…with a lion's head," suggested George.

"A white tiger, a white tiger, with a lion's head!" screeched Lancer.

Lancer gave a massive sigh, "Well you're not far off."

"I'm a Liger, my mother was a lion and my father was a tiger. I never knew either of them (he sighed further). I was raised by the grey squibbits and I work for their chief."

Billy was wondering what the liger would diet on if it wasn't eating the abundance of squibbits he knew inhabited the wood.

Billy continued to quiz Lancer, trying to work out the liger's weaknesses, if he had any. Billy, beginning to get used to the surprises of the wood was not going to be side tracked from his chosen mission. The boys were beginning to learn all about Lancer's personality and how proud he was about his skills. Lancer was happy to tell them how ligers usually die young but he was exceptionally strong.

Billy and George were trying to befriend the animal, Billy to strengthen their chances of deceiving him to further their aims and George because he feared he would be Lancer's next meal.

Lancer was really beginning to enjoy waxing lyrical about his extensive skills and talents. He went on to share with the listening twosome how he was four metres long, making him the largest cat in the world by nearly half-a-metre. His white fur was not explained by himself and Billy was not keen to upset him by being too personal, maybe he didn't know his fur was not normal. Lancer also bragged about how lion's cannot go swimming or see so well in the dark, but his father passed on these attributes to him through his tiger genes.

"My father, I imagine, was a great night hunter, as I can see in the labyrinth like I have night vision goggles and he must have been a mighty swimmer in the Jungle Olympics as I can out swim any cat you care to name."

Billy hadn't quite worked out how he was going to bypass this fine huge strapping feline.

"How fast can you run?" Billy continued his trek for fragility in the massive critter.

"Run, run! I am too heavy to run very far or for very long; I weigh half-a-ton," he continued.

Billy broke into a very tiny smile as he now felt he was gaining some kind of advantage and a plan began to form in his mind.

"I roam the labyrinth each day and feed from the squibbits offerings by the exits. I also get to eat anything I find in the labyrinth. Of course you know that lions and tigers sleep eighteen to twenty hours a day," Lancer informed them.

Billy was beginning to see that exploration of the labyrinth might just be possible still, even with this burly, loyal guardian.

"Do you get lonely?" Billy asked.

"Oh I do! Yes, Yes, it is a lonely job but I do get company from time to time," Lancer continued.

Lancer was saddened as he said, "It can be distressing when you chat away to something and you're just getting to know the creatures, much like yourselves, then you suddenly get hungry and I am forced to eat!"

"Well I can't stop here all day chatting, much as though you both smell quite tasty." With that Lancer popped himself back on his paws and strode back to disappear through the door.

Stopping to turn, the liger announced with a smile, "If you do go down in the labyrinth be sure to both come as one of you will only be a snack and in a few hours I am going to be well hungry!"

Lancer turned and vanished back into the Golden Shed and down into the labyrinth. The two boys picked themselves-up and George started to walk in the direction of home. George was snatched back by the collar and was yanked back by Billy.

"You're not leaving me; I can't do this alone!"

"For flip's sake Billy, I think it's your very worst idea ever!" protested George.

"You can't leave me, you're my wingman and I need you. You're my powerful side-kick, my trusty partner, my … well…my friend!" babbled Billy desperate for George to stay as he really couldn't go down on his own and be sure to survive.

When George heard the magic word – friend – he stopped protesting as he had never in his young life really had a best mate and now he had a really cool friend, a brave friend, perhaps crazy friend but definitely an exciting friend.

George thought for a moment and then decided he would try to buy in to Billy's plans. Billy showed him the contents of the black rucksack. He had just about everything you could possibly need to go searching a pitch black labyrinth. The contents of the bag included: two orange hard helmets with fully working headlights, torches, his smart phone, a massive ball of string and a rope ladder.

"My, my you have come prepared!" observed George.

The Golden Shed had been left-open by Lancer, who they assumed might be bad at his job. Perhaps he simply dashed off and forgot to close the door and windows as George suggested. Billy was silently apprehensive as it crossed his mind that it might just be a trap and that Lancer was inviting them in.

Billy fixed-up a lighted helmet for both of them and let the rope ladder down into the maze of darkened passages that beckoned. Billy threw his rucksack onto his back and started his descent into the dark with his friend following. They took a minute or so to reach the bottom and Billy tied the end of the huge ball of string to the rope ladder. The string would flow from the specially made hole in the rucksack and if all went to plan would be their way of finding their route back to the Golden Shed.

George took a minute, hands gripped to the rope ladder wondering if he really should let go. Then the intrepid pair were about to embark on a discovery that they were sure would be marvellous or just plain catastrophic.

As they shuffled around in the dark unknown they turned their head-mounted lights on and pondered which way to advance. Billy was still thinking, trying to measure up the white liger he had just made contact with. What was the white liger? A horrid hybrid or a friendly union of prime tiger and lovely lion? Lancer was essentially a member of Razor the Chief Squibbits' family, throng, circle of friends or as he had also hinted at ...his army!

Billy had only had very positive relations with Razor so far but he was Chief of all grey squibbits and he had, according to himself, fought battles to be the dominant species of the wood. Billy pondered how he would protect what he had worked so hard to gain. Was Razor really their friend or was he hiding something in the labyrinth? Something that he perhaps dare not risk the wider world knowing about? Was it such a coincidence that Razor found them to keep them talking and that Lancer was so keen about his duty on this day?

Billy started to have second thoughts but didn't share them with George. He was not willing to lose face in front of someone who he felt had come to look up to him and Billy was always keen to play the big brave man. Perfect as a specimen was Lancer, all white, flawless and immense it would be a tragedy if he had to kill it, thought Billy. He didn't question the fact that he might have to slay the liger or even think about how he might go about such a task, only that he might have to do it.

Lancer had made it clear that he intended to feed on both of them if they were to be found in the labyrinth but undeterred they continued.

Razor and some of his band of squibbits had watched the boys and Lancer from the shadows of the trees. Razor turned to a smaller squibbit as he listened and observed both the red and the blue lads from a far. "They have no fear these brave boys, but they have a ruck sack full of stupidity," Razor commented.

"Those boys could be useful to us. Prepare a half-bled deer and quarter it, then place each individual quarter at each compass entrance of the labyrinth. If Lancer does his job these boys will need our help...again!" Razor instructed his aid. His assistant that day was trusty Archer who would ensure that a quarter of a dead deer would be placed at each exit of the labyrinth but that might not be enough to lure Lancer away from his sport for he had a hearty appetite and was a greedy animal!

Found

Billy was fixing the rope ladder for the both of them to ease their way down. As they heard the end of the rope ladder hit the floor of the labyrinth a loud squawk rang out, and a huge magpie flew up from the abyss and flew out between their heads. George was convinced it tried to scratch them as it left the labyrinth.

Billy and George eased themselves down the rope ladder and were now slowly wandering into the labyrinth, almost pin knobbing as Billy he led his pal he knew not where. They dare not move too quickly for fear of a pouncing liger or a brand new but unpleasant surprise from this cavern of secrets. Billy realised that walking around the labyrinth was not his greatest problem. He had in his possession not one single item he could use as a weapon against a four-metre long liger. Despite the fact he was unarmed he was still confident he could kill Lancer- if he had to.

As they switched on their head lamps and torches they soon came across an interesting shiny stock pile.

"Look at this lot!" Billy squealed

"There's all sorts here!" he continued.

"Wow, a silver tea pot, silver tray, pearl necklace, a gold pocket watch and look at this! You know what this is don't you?"

Billy held the item up into the light for George to get a good look at it.

"It's the referee's whistle that the magpie stole!"

"Are you sure?" quizzed George.

"Look it has an inscription, EFL Referee's Official Whistle. It has to be!"

"This must all be stolen by that magpie." Billy insisted.

"Look at the size of this stuff. It couldn't be carried by a magpie bird," George suggested.

Billy offered another explanation, "The whistle and maybe a necklace but most of the other stuff? No, I agree. How about Mickey Magpie? This could be his lousy stash. He's out there somewhere!"

"Well let's not hang around he could be on his way back."

George suggested they could just go home; a suggestion to which Billy copped a deaf 'un and merely gestured him forward, deeper into the labyrinth.

The black maze was hugely complex. The string Billy had tied to the rope ladder was unravelling faster as they grew in confidence as their ears began to guide them just as sure as their eyes. This shaded puzzle was clearly designed to baffle the human mind and heart. They could get lost in their forever and so the string became their lifeline.

Dead-end after dead-end forced the two heroes back and forth never being quite sure where they had already been. The string was holding, 'thank goodness'. At last, by eliminating all the dead ends, they drew closer and closer to the centre, until they could hear the puffing and purring of a huge animal they were hoping to evade. They allowed the noise to pull them fearfully forward into the gloom. The closer they came, the worse the stench of discarded carcasses assailed their nostrils – the rotting waste of Lancer's victims.

Lancer had sensed the boys' entry into the labyrinth for some time catching their scent the moment they had set foot on the ground. The liger had waited for them to find him but was now lying, eyes resting with his tail actively creating the loud thudding. Snore, followed snore as the creature lay deep in slumber.

Billy and George were relieved to see Lancer's still state but Billy would be careful not to change that. Billy stood on his tip-toes as they started to edge passed the slumbering giant, with George in close attendance. They stuck to the wall of the labyrinth, their hands feeling along the surface of the wall. Once they had shuffled passed they began to stride confidently away from the guardian and down the next passage way.

"Is that light ahead?" George asked in hope.

Billy directed his eyes to the same venue as George's and confirmed, "You're right, that's sunlight."

The two boys continued to stride forward towards the light. The string had long run out but there was no turning back now. They were walking assertively towards fresh air and a cooling breeze. A great roar was suddenly upon them, a roar they had only to recently been introduced to. Lancer had stirred, he had caught the scent of the quartered deer placed at the entrances by the trusty Archer. Lancer had concluded that dinner was served and little boys would make a great dessert!

He was now savouring the aroma of the boys and the deer so was working his way with giant strides towards them. The liger might not have been much of a runner but his strides were long. The feline fiend was catching the boys quickly as he broke into a trot.

The two boys began to sprint towards the light and breeze as fast as they could manage, as half a ton of cat was thudding down the passage towards them.

Thud....thud....thud...thud...thud..thud..thud.thud.thud.thud. It was now a gallop, a loping, long, striding gallop!

George tripped on a stone and fell flat on his face. He was struggling to get to his feet on the dusty dirt surface. An arm of mud reached out of the base of the labyrinths wall and made a grab for George's leg and gripped it tightly trying to strangle the veins out of his limb.

George was sure he was a goner and prepared himself to be gorged on by the hulking cat!

On realising his pal's peril, without hesitation, Billy threw his rucksack towards the direction of Lancer, kicked the arm and then stamped on it hard.

By now the helmets had abandoned their head and as the arm retracted in pain, George was able to spring to his feet for them both to resume their scrambled and desperate escape bolt.

"Stay in the middle of the path! We're nearly out and then follow me," Billy instructed.

At the exit of the labyrinth stood a knife wielding Mickey Magpie who had just started to eat the raw quartered deer left for the chasing Lancer. His hands were covered in blood and so was his knife where he had cut himself a slice of raw venison. Mickey Magpie turned to face the dynamic running duo and his knife glinted as the sun caught its' blade.

Lancer continued to roar and the labyrinth started to shake. In blind panic and his heart running faster than both of them George was crying inside as he saw the familiar figure at the end of the tunnel blocking the light that had recently shone so brightly.

Billy then clocked the figure as well, "Duck under his arms and mind his knives!"

The boys were running faster and faster as the mystical powers of the labyrinth gave them the speed of a locomotive. George ducked under Mickey Magpie's grasping arm as he skipped over the bleeding deer; Billy dived between his legs before continuing his sprint. The two boys were out of the dark and into the pelting sunshine as they ran to the nearest massive tree and climbed like a pair of super strong chimps!

They both heard a man's chilling cry and a huge thump of a heavy weight hitting the floor.

The two of them climbed the tree like a ladder, seemingly confident they would, at least for a time, be safe. It was a very large oak tree strong and over a century old. They clawed their way skywards, some ten metres high. They then looked at the entrance to the dark maze and saw Lancer retracting his bloodied claws from the body of Mickey Magpie who lay on the ground motionless and surrounded in a pool of red juice!

The two boys stared as Lancer ripped his teeth into the neck of the former member of the World Infamous Crow Gang!

Canines and incisors were flashing in the sun and slashing on the meat as the uncooked flesh was devoured.

Billy and George realised that Lancer had almost certainly saved their lives!

"What now?" queried George.

"Well I think we should stay here for a bit, get our breath back and just watch that liger over there have its' fill," replied Billy.

As they both watched Lancer do a vanishing trick with magpie meat, George agreed that resting in the tree was the best idea for now. George thanked Billy for saving him and was quite concerned that he'd lost his rucksack in the melee. Billy just shrugged his shoulders.

George was calming down now and felt guilty that he actually felt delighted that Mickey Magpie was no more! He commented it was getting late and they were due home soon, Billy agreed with him.

"How are we going to get home from here?" asked George.

"I don't know…yet." Billy had started to scan the landscape from his lofty perch hoping to spot a familiar landmark. He was hoping to spot the Golden Shed which he thought was their best hope for a clear route home. Fortunately, he could see the Sun bouncing off the Golden Shed but then he realised where they were. Billy spotted a major problem but for him a pleasant handicap. Billy started to laugh.

"Take a look. Go on George, just take a look!" Billy was pointing in the direction of Wobbling Wood.

"Oh, I see what you mean," George said confused.

Running through the wood and beginning by the side of the exit of the labyrinth was the huge outer wall of Skaggyness. The two boys were out of bounds!

For the very first time George was free from the unexplained grip of the walls of Skaggyness which had been present in his life a full ten man years.

"My dad won't like this; he'll go ballistic when he finds out!"

"When he finds out? Don't you mean IF he finds out?" Billy highlighted the less certain nature of the problem.

"How will he find out?" quizzed Billy.

Billy continued, "Nobody needs to even know we were ever in Wobbling Wood, let alone on the outside of the wall. Look we are cleaner now than when we came in and I feel like I've got energy for a whole new day."

"That Labyrinth certainly has spirits unknown. I mean that arm, what was that all about? Where did it come from?" canvassed George.

"I don't think we've even begun to discover the secrets of that labyrinth or the wood!" Billy asserted.

George reminded Billy that it was school on Monday and that it was probably 'it' for adventure, at least until the next holiday. George reminded Billy they had something called weekends, Billy agreed but reminded him that family, football and homework have always come first on the weekend for him.

The two boys were stuck up the tree for some time and the evening was creeping towards them. The colourful pair monitored Lancer settling himself down into the exit of the maze of tunnels. They watched Mickey Magpies head roll across the grass as Lancer was still munching his ample meal. The Sun, way out on the horizon, started to lower itself into the sea.

It wasn't too long before they heard the sound of Lancer's loud purring and the relaxed nature of the gentle thudding of his tail. "He's asleep!" uttered Billy.

Lancer was some distance from the tree and this was their chance to start to move towards home. They gently eased themselves down the branches of the tree and were ever so accurate in their planning of the gentle steps they chose as they found the ground. They moved with caution as they gently strolled away from the slumbering ogre and towards where they believed the road home was to be found. They were following the outer wall searching for the road that would lead them back into Skaggyness and familiar surroundings.

As they made progress towards a noise of road traffic, they glanced over their shoulders to spy the sleeping white paws of their past pursuer. As they turned back George spied another familiar creature.

"Random!" blurted George and promptly ran towards the roaming white horse.

Taken aback, Billy wondered how George would know the name of, what appeared to him, to be a stray horse. As it sauntered over to them both, he observed how affectionate George was towards the horse. George had needed to hug something after all the excitement and Random was clearly enjoying the pats and hugs of his companion.

Curiously, Billy enquired how he knew the ivory shade of nag. "This is Random! He's just Random! He has the freedom of Skaggyness and goes anywhere in the town he likes," explained George. Billy was contemplating this idea of a white horse just meandering around Skaggyness. Why ever has he been allowed to do that? Billy had never come across this before; all stray animals are collected by the R.S.P.C.A. as far as he knew. "Don't the police or someone come and deal with him?" queried Billy.

Anxiously, recalling his recent witnessing of police action of capturing the now deceased Mickey Magpie outside of his home, George reacted,

"The police! Why? Why would they ever come for Random?" Billy noted how protective of the steed he was, clearly having great devotion to the animal.

"We are not allowed pets in our house, so when random wanders in my path I like to make a fuss. He has always been around Skaggyness and regularly wanders into Wibble Street. I have known him since I was a little boy," George affirmed.

Billy stood back slightly to take a closer survey of Random. He noted that he was a creature to behold with an athletic physique. Random had sturdy looking shoulders and not an ounce of fat was upon this superb glowing stallion. The fact that the horse wasn't claimed or allowed to roam where it pleased was not apparent but still Billy had noted the boy's quickest route home.

"He's a strong horse isn't he?" said Billy in admiration.

"Very!" agreed George.

Calmly, Billy requested further information as to George's knowledge of the horse.

"Have you ever ridden him?"

"Ridden him?"

"Yes, can you ride this horse?"

"Well, I have never tried and I have never seen him being ridden by anyone. I have never seen a saddle on him, he just wanders," George briefed his friend.

Realising what Billy was thinking George protested,

"Oh no! No, no! I have had enough danger for one day. I'm not going to break my back falling off my favourite horse."

Billy tried to play on George's accord with the snowy steed.

"I think this horse will let you ride him and I also think he will get us both back to Wibble Street."

Defensively, "I don't want to hurt him," George continued to air his outcry.

"Mate, seriously, take a look at your horse. He's a strapping sturdy animal. He's got muscles everywhere. He can take two featherweight lads. We can ride him bare back," Billy proposed.

George knew it was pointless staging any further protest as Billy always seemed to get his way and deep down George just wanted to get back to familiar territory.

Maybe Billy is right? Maybe random is the quickest way home mused

George to himself.

Billy was totally sure that George would soon capitulate in his protests as he was absolutely convinced that he would soon fall in love with the very idea of riding this animal that had clearly earned his utter devotion.

"How will I get on him?" asked George.

A vast smirk broke out onto Billy's face, "Hold onto his mane and I'll give you a leg-up. When you're on just give me a hand-up."

Billy made his hands into a stirrup for George to use and climb on the patient Random. When comfortable, George offered his hand to Billy and used all his strength to lift him on.

Random never moved a muscle and the two equestrian novices sat astride the gentle giant.

"What do we do now?" asked George.

The two boys sat silently, each waiting for the other to utter some kind of magic sentence.

Both tried to give a kick to Randoms' belly in the hope they at least would move forward. Random was busy grazing on the lush long grass in front of him, head stooped oblivious to the riders kicking.

"Squeeze his body with your knees," Billy suggested. Still no response.

Frantically, Billy started to bellow, "Giddy up, giddy up!" whilst still kicking and squeezing; all to no avail.

When Random was ready he stepped forward and then another step. He raised his head. When the boys stopped trying to control him he began to move forward ever so mildly and steadily. Random lifted his head and appeared to sniff the air and look around him. Random altered his position and started to walk in a definite direction.

As the road began to show itself to the boys, Billy pinched George and suggested that they were on the way home. As Random reached the road he turned and started to trot on the grass that lay beside the carriageway.

George spotted a road sign which read, 'Skaggyness three miles'. He dug his elbow into Billy's ribs and Billy patted his shoulder to let him know he'd seen it.

Random appeared to look at the sign as well and as they passed it his motion increased to a canter.

The two boys gripped the animal tighter as it increased its' speed. In minutes the boys were reduced down to a walk again as they arrived in what felt liked triumph through the entrance to Skaggyness. Facing them was the Olympic hypermarket and they were in the very spot where inexplicably George had been hauled off the pink bike.

Random continued a gentle walk into Twilight Street and half-way down came to a halt. Random went down onto his front and the two mates slid southwards to a safe dismount. George and Billy patted Random to give thanks. Random paused for their gratitude before turning back to head back down Twilight Street.

George was deliriously waving and shouting messages of thanks to Random as the equine explorer disappeared around the corner. Billy was standing watching shaking his head after another unbelievable day.

The two boys reached the corner of Wibble Street by George's scarlet home.

"Well I guess that's the end of the summer fun then," Billy sighed.

"Erm, guess so," uttered George in agreement.

Billy was already contemplating a return visit to Wobbling Wood at the very first opportunity. Billy explained that he was going to be dragged around the Olympic hypermarket the next day. He would be shopping for the new school term and with that he headed back to number eleven. George noted that his dad's car was in the drive.

He knocked, being careful not to beat the door too loudly and waited to be allowed to go in. He waited and he waited some more. His dad would let him in eventually and until then he was all alone again. He was used to being on his own but he didn't like it any more.

The door eventually flung open and a burly command of "In!" was forthcoming.

George kept his head down as he squeezed passed his father as he went in search of a hug from his mum, food for his belly and a warm, safe bed.

ABOUT THE AUTHOR

After his first taste of teaching in Poznan, Poland the author has influenced and advanced the basic skills of children and adults alike in numerous academic centres.

Teaching has taken him to France, Poland, Russia, Saudi Arabia, Spain, Switzerland and Taiwan – as well as many areas of the UK.

He gained a PGCE in Primary Education after training at Bishops Grosseteste College, Lincoln adding to his numerous teaching qualifications. Andrew William gained a Masters Degree in Education from The Open University prior to undertaking a formal teaching position.

The characters and stories of Wibble Street are a product of the stories he first shared with pupils in his classes during his time as an NQT in Skegness and then throughout his career.

He is originally from Burton-upon-Trent, Staffordshire and now lives there once again. He currently holds teaching positions in both Derby and Burton-upon-Trent.

Made in the USA
Columbia, SC
19 January 2018